THE GUNSMITH

#24

KILLER GRIZZLY

Other Books
By
J.R. Roberts

Macklin's Women
The Chinese Gunmen
The Woman Hunt
The Guns of Abilene
Three Guns for Glory
Leadtown
The Longhorn War
Quanah's Revenge
Heavyweight Gun
New Orleans Fire
One-Handed Gun
The Canadian Payroll
Draw to an Inside Death
Dead Man's Hand
Bandit Gold
Buckskins and Six-Guns
Silver War
High Noon at Lancaster
Bandido Blood
The Dodge City Gang
Sasquatch Hunt
Bullets and Ballots
The Riverboat Gang
Killer Grizzly
North of the Border
Eagle's Gap

Chinatown Hell
The Panhandle Search
Wildcat Roundup
The Ponderosa War
Trouble Rides a Fast Horse
Dynamite Justice
The Posse
Night of the Gila
The Bounty Women
Black Pearl Saloon
Gundown in Paradise
King of the Border
The El Paso Salt War
The Ten Pines Killer
Hell with a Pistol
Wyoming Cattle Kill
The Golden Horseman
The Scarlet Gun
Navaho Devil
Wild Bill's Ghost
The Miner's Showdown
Archer's Revenge
Showdown in Raton
When Legends Meet
Desert Hell
The Diamond Gun

For more exciting
E-Books, Audiobooks and MP3 downloads visit us at
www.speakingvolumes.us

THE GUNSMITH

#24

KILLER GRIZZLY

J.R. ROBERTS

SPEAKING VOLUMES, LLC
NAPLES, FLORIDA
2013

THE GUNSMITH
#24 KILLER GRIZZLY

ISBN 978-1-61232-627-6

Chapter One

When the left rear wheel on the Gunsmith's rig broke there was an audible snap, and then the wagon began to list to the left.

"Damn!" Clint Adams muttered wearily. He had tensed to jump free in case the whole rig started to go, but when there was no apparent danger of that he relaxed. *Thank God for small favors*, he thought and dropped lightly to the ground.

One glance told him that nothing short of a new wheel was going to get them going again.

"Well, Duke, boy," he said, approaching his big, black gelding, "it looks like you and me have got to ride to the nearest town for help."

Clint checked the padlock on the rear door of his rig, but he knew that if anyone wanted to get inside bad enough, his gunsmithing equipment would be easy pickings out here in the middle of nowhere.

"Let's go, big boy," he said, freeing Duke's reins. "The sooner we get going, the sooner we'll get this wheel fixed so we can be on our way."

With a last, longing look at his rig, containing all of his worldly possessions, he swung easily into the saddle and headed north, hoping that the next town wasn't in Montana.

"A reward is out of the question!" Benjamin Slade, the mayor of Bear Pass, Wyoming said. He was addressing the town council, and the subject was a grizzly not so affectionately known as "Ol' Three-Paw."

"You have no say in the matter," Calvin Lockman retorted. "The money is mine, not the town's. Besides, I'm sure if we put it to a vote the majority of this council would side with me. If we did that, the money would come from the town."

Slade glowered at Lockman, but he knew the man was right. Calvin Lockman owned the largest ranch in the county, and his word carried a lot of weight. If the mayor opposed him, all he'd succeed in doing would be to hinder any chance of re-election in three months.

Still, token resistance was expected.

"Offering a reward for this animal will attract all sorts of undesirables to Bear Pass," he said.

"If one of them can get rid of Ol' Three-Paw," another council member said, "they're all welcome."

Ol' Three-Paw was a monstrous grizzly who had been terrorizing the surrounding area for months. To date he had accounted for the deaths of sheep, cattle, horses and three men. The animal had not yet struck close to the town, but how long would it be before he got that bold? So far, he'd had everything his own way. Several hunting parties comprised of ranch hands and townspeople had gone out after him, but they invariably came back swearing that the creature had an almost human intelligence. At times they even swore that the grizzly had been taunting them.

"Now, I'm not going to put this to a vote," Lockman said to the council in general. "I'm offering five thousand dollars to anyone who can bring me proof that they've killed that animal."

"Where will this offer appear?" the mayor asked.

"I'll have posters made up," Lockman said, "and it will be run in the newspapers."

Mayor Slade shook his head, but kept any further protestations to himself.

"Any objections?" Lockman asked. There were none. "Then with a little luck, Ol' Three-Paw should be dead within a week."

Within a week, Slade thought, *the area will be crawling with hunters—professionals as well as amateurs—shooting at anything that moves.*

As the meeting broke up and the council members began to leave Lockman approached Slade and said, "Ben, could we talk in your office?"

"Of course, Calvin," Slade said. "We'll have some of that fine brandy you gave me."

When they were both seated in the mayor's office holding snifters of Lockman's imported brandy, Slade settled back to hear what Lockman had to say.

Ben Slade was a failed politician in his early fifties who was desperate to hold on to his job as mayor of Bear Pass. It wasn't much, but it was the last position he'd ever hold, of that he was sure, and he wanted to hold it as long as possible, even if it meant eating Calvin Lockman's shit.

Calvin Lockman was in his late thirties, and already had more money than any man could ever need. That did not, however, diminish his lust for more money and more power.

"Benjamin," Lockman began, "I would not advise that you ever speak up against me like that again when we're meeting with the town council."

"They expect me to make some sort of effort—"

"That's fine, Benjamin," Lockman said, cutting him off, "but not on this matter. This grizzly must be destroyed."

"I agree with you there, Calvin," Slade said, "but what I don't agree with is your method."

"That's neither here nor there. Whether you agree or not, I will take whatever measures necessary to see that this animal threatens us no longer." Lockman finished his brandy and stood up.

"I just hope that too many amateur hunters don't reply to this reward of yours," Slade said. "The last thing we need is a bunch of people with guns running around shooting at the first thing that moves."

"I'm sure that we'll get a couple of professionals to respond to the reward," Lockman said. "I've already tried to hire a couple, but they were either busy, or they just didn't want any part of Ol' Three-Paw."

"I suppose his reputation has preceded him," Slade remarked.

"And as his reputation grows, this town's diminishes," Lockman said. "We can't have that, Benjamin. Believe me, I'm doing the right thing."

"I hope so, Calvin," Slade said, pouring himself another glass of brandy. Lately, he'd been drinking quite a bit of the stuff—and rot-gut whiskey when he ran out—and Lockman noticed that the bottle was almost empty.

"Running low, I see, Benjamin," Lockman said. "I'll have another batch delivered to you this afternoon. I know how you enjoy your brandy."

"Yes, I do," Slade said, lifting his glass to examine the contents. "I appreciate it, Calvin."

"I'm sure you do, Benjamin," Lockman said. "I'll get you some more before that runs out. I wouldn't want you to have to face the day without it."

Slade started to lift his glass in a silent toast, but noticed that it was empty again. He was filling it as Calvin Lockman was going out the door.

"Bear Pass," Clint read aloud from the makeshift signpost. There was no indication of population. "Hell of a name for a town, huh, Duke?"

At that point the big horse's head came up and he cocked his ears. Clint felt a rumbling start inside Duke's chest and knew that something was bothering him.

"What is it, big fella?" Clint asked, patting Duke's massive neck.

Duke's head came up higher, as if he were listening, or even sniffing at the air. It was pretty damn sure that he either heard or smelled something that he didn't like, and Clint began to look around, patting Duke's neck all the while.

And then he saw it.

It was easily the biggest grizzly Clint had ever seen. It was far enough away to make an accurate guess at its size impossible, but it was near enough for Duke to have gotten wind of it.

"Okay, big guy, I see it," Clint said.

It was atop a hill, standing up on its hind paws, and it seemed to be watching them.

"It's no danger to us while it stays that far away," Clint told Duke, rubbing his neck, "and if it starts towards us you can easily outrun it. Let's just move on nice and easy, okay?'' he said, nudging the big horse's ribs with his boot heels. Duke's muscles were tensed, but he responded to Clint's gentle handling and began to move forward at a walk.

Clint looked back and saw the grizzly still watching them. *God*, he thought, *just how big is that son of a bitch?*

Chapter Two

By the time Clint and Duke rode into Bear Pass the big horse still had not fully relaxed.

"We'll get you some feed and a good rubdown, big boy, and you'll be fine. I don't blame you."

Clint stopped a man in the street and asked directions to the livery, then proceeded directly there, even though his mouth and throat were screaming out for a drink.

When he reached the livery stable he dismounted and walked Duke in.

"Anybody here?" he shouted.

"Yo!" came a reply from the back. A strapping man of about thirty, with huge forearms and shoulders, came out of a back office, wiping his hands on a dirty cloth.

"What can I do for you—" he started to ask, but when his eyes fell on Duke he was struck silent. He pursed his lips and let out an admiring whistle.

"What an animal!" he said.

"He needs some feed and a rub," Clint said.

"Be my pleasure, mister," the man said.

"I've also got a wheel on a rig that needs replacing," Clint added.

"Where is it?"

7

"About a mile north of town. Can you go out there and fix it for me?"

"Have to charge you hazard pay," the man replied.

"Hazard pay?" Clint asked. "For what?"

"Ol' Three-Paw's roaming around out there," the man answered. "If you want me to go out there alone to fix your wagon, you're gonna have to make it worth my while."

"Three-Paw?" Clint asked. "You wouldn't be referring to a big grizzly, would you?"

"You heard of him?"

"No, but I've seen him."

The admiring look on the man's face turned to one of awe and he moved his eyes from Duke to the Gunsmith.

"You saw him? Where?"

"Just outside of town, by a signpost. He was up on a hill, standing upright."

"Jesus!" the man said, swallowing hard. "That's the closest anybody's ever seen him to town! I gotta tell the sheriff!"

Clint put out a hand to stop the man before he could run out into the street. "I'll tell you what. *I'll* tell the sheriff, and you take care of my horse. Then you can get out there, take care of my wheel, and bring in my team and rig."

"You left your team out there?" the man asked. "Jesus, mister, they ain't got a prayer—"

"How the hell was I supposed to know there was a grizzly running around out there?" Clint shot back. "Hell, I didn't even know I was this close to a town until I saw the signpost."

"Mister, it'll be my pleasure to take care of your horse," the man said, "but about going out there to fix your rig—"

"Look, almost everything I own is in that rig, except for what I've got on me," Clint said. "You be ready to go and I'll go out there with you and ride shotgun. Have another horse ready for me, will you?"

"Another horse?"

"I'll rent it from you," Clint assured him, "and I'll give you your hazard pay. Just get me a wheel, okay?"

"You've got it."

Clint handed the man the reins and said, "Take good care of him. I'll be right back as soon as I get a drink and talk to the sheriff."

"Sheriff's office is right down the street, to the right."

"What's his name?"

"Joe Hanson."

"Thanks."

As Clint headed for the sheriff's office his mind was on his team, and that great big grizzly. He hoped they'd be all right but he couldn't help feeling sorry that he'd left them hitched to the wagon. If that grizzly decided to pay them a visit, they'd be easy pickings.

How could he have known there was a grizzly? he asked himself again. The answer was, he couldn't, so he might as well just stop thinking about it.

He decided to forget about getting a drink and go right back to the livery after talking to the sheriff. The faster he got back to his rig, the better chance the team had of making it.

Chapter Three

The rig was still there when Clint and the liveryman—whose name was Hank—got back out there, but now it was lying on its side, and the bloody carcasses lying in front of it, still hitched to it, no longer resembled what had once been the Gunsmith's team.

"Jesus," Hank said in awe.

"Christ," the Gunsmith added.

The mutilated bodies were no longer even vaguely recognizable as horses, and that one creature could do that to two animals who weighed a combined four thousand pounds or so was frightening.

Earlier, in Bear Pass, Clint had walked in on Sheriff Joe Hanson while the lawman was enjoying a cup of coffee, and after the Gunsmith identified himself, the sheriff invited him to join him.

"It's a pleasure to make your acquaintance," Hanson said with sincerity. "What brings you to Bear Pass?"

"A broken wheel," Clint answered, and went on to explain his predicament.

"Well, Hank's a good man," Hanson assured him.

"He'll fix it, all right . . . if you can get him out there."

"I told him I'd ride shotgun," Clint explained, "and pay him extra."

"That ought to do it," Hanson agreed. He put his coffee cup down with a sigh and said, "I guess I'll have to let the mayor and the town council know that Ol' Three-Paw was spotted that close to town. I just hope it doesn't start a panic. That's the last thing we need."

"Don't let it get around, then," Clint suggested, finishing his coffee. "I'm sure you can keep it between you and the mayor and the council."

"You were a lawman," Hanson said. "You've dealt with situations like this. Bad news always has a way of getting out."

"That's true." Both men stood up and Clint said, "I guess I'd better get back to Hank and get my wheel fixed. The sooner I get my team and rig into town, the better I'll feel."

"Can't blame you for that," Hanson said. They left the office together and went their separate ways. When Clint got back to the livery Hank was ready with a buckboard, spare wheel, and another horse for Clint.

"Before we get started," Hank had said, "could we settle up?"

"You want to be paid in advance?"

Hank shrugged his massive shoulders and said, "With Ol' Three-Paw out there, there's no tellin' what could happen."

"He can't be much bigger than you," Clint complained, digging into his pocket.

"I ain't never backed away from a fight, mister, but I wouldn't tangle with that grizzly on a bet."

"Half now, and half when we get back," Clint said, handing Hank some bills.

"Sold."

Now, with the team dead and the wagon lying on its side, Hank was starting to wish he'd held out for more.

"This is gonna take longer than I thought," Hank complained, looking around for Ol' Three-Paw.

"We made a deal, Hank," Clint reminded him. "We'll unhitch the dead team, right the wagon and then fix the wheel. Then we'll hitch this horse to my rig and take it back to town. Simple."

"Sure," Hank said, "if Ol' Three-Paw don't come back."

"If he comes back, we'll bag him," Clint said. "I've got enough guns in my rig, we can come up with one big enough to do the job."

"I've heard that before," Hank said.

"You can tell me all your grizzly stories while we work on the wheel," Clint said, "and you can start with why he's called Ol' Three-Paw."

While they freed the rig from the carcasses and used a horse, a rope, a tree and some leverage to right it, Hank told Clint the story of the only time Ol' Three-Paw even came close to getting caught. One of the ranchers got the idea of laying out bear traps, and the grizzly actually stepped in one.

"What happened?"

"That mean grizzly chewed off his own paw and got away," Hank explained.

"Which explains why he's called Ol' Three-Paw," Clint said.

"Right."

"That must be one mean son of a bitch," Clint said, shaking his head.

"And smart," Hank said. "After that, they found all the rest of the traps tripped."

"You mean that grizzly was smart enough to spring the rest of the traps without getting caught in them?"

"That's what they say," Hank answered.

Clint knew better than most that what people "say" is what builds legends. The only thing he was sure of was that this grizzly was big and dangerous, and that was because he had seen that much with his own eyes. For the rest, he'd just have to wait and see how much could be verified.

It took them a while, but they finally managed to get the rig ready to roll and hitched up to Clint's horse for the ride to town.

"You lead the way," Clint said, climbing up into the seat of his rig. "I'll follow you in."

"Just keep your gun handy, mister," Hank said, and then added, "and your money."

"Just worry about selling me two good horses to replace my team," Clint told him, "and at a good price."

"I just hope we get back to town alive so we can haggle."

When they finally got back to town Clint figured it was time for that drink, and he invited Hank to join him.

"I don't mind telling you I need one," the livery-man replied.

"And you deserve it," Clint said. "I appreciate what you did for me today, Hank. It took guts."

"Not really," Hank replied, looking sheepish at the

praise. "I'd do almost anything for money—leastways, that's what folks in town say."

"You can tell me why they say that over that drink," Clint told him. "Where's the best saloon in town?"

"Right this way."

Chapter Four

Hank's last name was Pride and, he explained, people in town paid him to perform feats of strength.

"See, I'm pretty strong," Hank added.

"I noticed," Clint said. He had seen the way Hank's arms bulged when they were lifting his rig up off its side, and when they were moving the heavy carcasses of the dead animals.

"Yeah, well, I was born in this town, before it was called Bear Pass, and ever since I was a kid, folks have been paying to see me lift this or move that, you know?"

"Anybody offer you money to wrestle a grizzly?" Clint asked.

Hank had been lifting his glass towards his mouth, and stopped short.

"Any other grizzly, maybe," he said, "but not Ol' Three-Paw. He ain't an ordinary grizzly."

"So I've been hearing."

"Anybody in this town'll tell you that," Hank said.

"I'll bet there are a lot of Ol' Three-Paw stories in this town," Clint said.

"Plenty," Hank agreed.

"But how many people have really seen him?" Clint asked. "I mean, up close."

Hank frowned and asked, "Why?"

"Just curious," Clint said. "I'd like to talk to someone who's really been close to this . . . monster."

"You ain't thinkin' about going after him, are you?" Hank asked.

"Well, he did cost me a pretty good team," Clint said. Of course, Clint felt bad about the two horses, but it was not as if he had lost Duke. The horses in the team changed from time to time, but Duke had been with Clint since he was a yearling. Losing him would have been a tremendous tragedy. Losing the team was little more than an inconvenience.

"That's crazy," Hank said. "Mister, that's just plain crazy thinking. Nobody goes out after that grizzly alone."

Hank still didn't know Clint's name, or his reputation, otherwise he might not have made that statement, but Clint saw no reason to enlighten the man. As it stood, they were just a couple of guys talking over a few drinks. Clint knew from past experience how that would change if Hank Pride found out that he was talking to the Gunsmith.

"Relax, Hank," Clint said. "I don't plan to be around that long, anyway."

"What are your plans?"

"Well, I'll stay the night, that's for sure, so I guess I'll have to get myself a hotel room. After that, I'll have to check out the damage to my rig and to my equipment."

"What kind of equipment?"

"I'm a gunsmith," Clint said.

"That's what you meant by having a lot of guns in your wagon," Hank observed.

"Right," Clint said. He stood up and dropped some

money on the table, and as Hank started to follow he said, "There's enough there for a few more drinks, Hank. Why don't you relax and use it up?"

Hank paused as he was starting to stand, then sat back down and asked, "You sure you don't want to see me bend a two-bit piece with my fingers, or something?"

"You've done enough for one day," Clint said. "Just relax. Maybe I'll see you later, when I check out my rig."

"I'll be around," Hank said.

"What hotel should I go to?"

"Go out and make a left, walk two blocks to the Montana House."

"Montana?"

Hank shrugged and said, "That's where the owner was headed when he decided to settle here—at least, that's the story I heard."

"Never mind," Clint said. "I've had enough stories for one day. See you later."

Clint left the saloon carrying his saddlebags and rifle and headed for the hotel. A hot bath was on his mind, but it would have to wait until later. He intended to get himself a room, drop off his stuff, and then check out the damage to his equipment and rig. If it was bad enough, it would probably keep him in town longer than he planned—considering he hadn't planned on stopping in Bear Pass at all.

"Wait a minute," Calvin Lockman told the mayor and the sheriff. "Wait a minute, there are two ways of looking at this."

"What are you talking about?" Slade asked. "That

monster has finally come within spitting distance of this town. If that gets out, it could turn us into a ghost town.''

After Sheriff Hanson had gone to Mayor Slade with the information, Slade had suggested they ride out to Lockman's place and tell him, which is where they were at the moment.

''The Gunsmith,'' Hanson said.

''What?'' Slade asked, switching his gaze from Lockman to the sheriff, and then back again. ''What did he say?''

''The Gunsmith is in town,'' Lockman said.

''Yeah, so?'' Slade asked. ''There's a gunfighter in town, so what? You gonna get Ol' Three-Paw to strap on a gun and step into the street with him?''

''The Gunsmith is more than that, Slade,'' Lockman said. ''You're beginning to panic and it's clouding your thinking.''

''Oh, yeah? I suppose I don't have any reason to panic,'' Slade said. ''Is that what you're telling me?''

''Exactly,'' Lockman said. ''Drink your brandy, Slade, and let me talk to Hanson.''

Slade looked as if he wanted to argue, then changed his mind and stuck his mouth inside a glass of brandy.

''Hanson, you know we have to keep this quiet,'' Lockman said.

''For how long?'' the lawman asked. ''How long do you think it will be before somebody else sees him?''

''We'll worry about that when the time comes,'' Lockman said. ''Look, the reward story hits the street tomorrow, and I've got newspapers all over Wyoming picking it up, and some in Montana too. Who knows how much farther it will go from there?''

''Too far.''

"Don't get like Slade," Lockman said. "We can get a head start on the reward story by talking to the Gunsmith now."

"You want to hire him to hunt down Ol' Three-Paw?"

"Why not? He was a lawman, a manhunter. What's the big difference between hunting a man and hunting an animal? It should be easier hunting down an animal, shouldn't it?"

"Not this animal," Hanson said.

"Look," Lockman said, ignoring Hanson's remark, "you get him to come out here and see me, and I'll do the rest."

Hanson shook his head and said, "I don't think he'd do it."

"What has he been doing since he quit being a lawman?" Lockman asked.

"I don't know," Hanson said. "I've heard about him from time to time. I guess he's been traveling."

"Sure, traveling," Lockman said. "Do you think he's been making money?"

Hanson gave a derisive laugh and said, "I never knew a lawman who did." Hanson was in his forties and had been a lawman for twenty years, and he had no bank account. He lived day to day on his salary, meager as it was, and long ago he had resigned himself to the fact that he'd never have money.

"Well, when I tell him how much this grizzly is worth to him dead, he'll remember that," Lockman said. "You get him here, Hanson, and I'll get him interested."

"Why not pull the reward, then?" Hanson asked.

"Oh, no," Lockman said. "That stands. All I'm doing with Adams is hedging my bet. Now you get him here," Lockman said, and then with a glance at a drunken Mayor Slade he added, "And while you're at it, get *him* out of here."

Chapter Five

When Clint returned to the livery Hank Pride was already there, lying underneath the rig.

"Hey, who's that?" the liveryman shouted when he heard footsteps. He crawled out from beneath the wagon and when he spotted Clint something on his face conveyed a message. Clint was sure that since the last time they'd spoken, Hank had found out who he was.

"Oh, uh, mister, uh—" Hank stammered.

"Clint will do," Clint told him. "Who'd you talk to?"

"What do you mean?"

"You obviously know who I am," Clint said, "and since I never formally introduced myself, you must have found out from someone. The sheriff?"

"Well," Hank said, "the bartender, but he found out from the sheriff."

"Hank, there's no reason to be nervous just because you found out my name," Clint said.

"I'm not—well, I am . . . a little. It's just that I never met anyone like you before."

"I'm just like anyone else," Clint assured him. "How's the rig look?"

"Oh, uh, I just thought since I got back before you that I'd take a look—I didn't try to go inside—"

"Hank, will you relax?" Clint cut in. "I know you

didn't try to get inside, and I appreciate you looking at the rig for me. Take it easy and just tell me what you found."

Hank nodded, seemed to make an effort to compose himself, and then said, "The front looks okay, but I found a small stress fracture on the rear axle. Must have happened when you hit whatever you hit to break the wheel."

"I didn't hit anything," Clint said, thinking back. "It just broke."

"No, you hit something, sometime, and didn't think anything of it. The wheel went first, but that axle would have gone pretty soon too."

"Well, then, it's a good thing you looked it over instead of me. I probably wouldn't have noticed the fracture, and would have gotten stuck again after leaving Bear Pass. You helped me out again, Hank."

"I, uh, just happened to spot it," Hank said. He was obviously unused to any kind of praise.

"Can you fix it?"

"I could, but you'd be better off if I replaced it," Hank said.

"How long would that take?"

"I'd have to send for the axle," Hank said. "Probably take a couple of days to get here. I could probably have it ready for you to leave in a few days."

"Three days in Bear Pass, huh?" Clint mused.

"There are worse places," Hank said. "We got a whorehouse and everything."

"Mmm," Clint said, but he wasn't thinking about women at that moment.

"You're thinking about that damn bear, ain't you?"

"Yeah, you're right, Hank," Clint replied. "I'm

thinking about that bear. It wouldn't hurt to go out and take a look at him, just while I'm here.''

"Don't count on that," Hank said. "It could hurt a lot."

"Order the part you need, Hank," Clint said. "I'm sure I can find something to do while I'm in town."

"I told you about the whorehouse—''

"If there's one thing I never do," Clint explained, "it's pay a woman to do something that should come natural. I'd just as soon sit down and play poker."

"Well, you'll find plenty of that around town too," Hank said.

"That's good to know," Clint said, "but I think I'll go back to the hotel, take a look at my room, and take a bath."

"Why?'' Hank asked, screwing his face up in an effort to understand why a man would *want* to take a bath.

"It's relaxing, Hank."

"Sitting in a tub full of water?'' Hank seemed to shiver and added, "Just thinking about it gives me the willies.''

"Well, you think about it and I'll go and do it."

"Better you than me," Hank said, and crawled back underneath the rig.

During the walk back to the hotel Clint found that he was virtually unable to keep himself from thinking about the beast everyone called Ol' Three-Paw. Call it curiosity, or fascination, or whatever, but the Gunsmith very much wanted a close-up look at that bear.

Chapter Six

The first time Clint had gone to the Montana House there had been a nattily dressed little man behind the counter. Clint had registered and asked that his belongings be put in his room.

Now as he entered the lobby he saw that the little man had been replaced by a woman—a tall, chestnut-haired, wide-shouldered, big-breasted woman.

She noticed him, too, as soon as he walked in.

"Can I help you, stranger?" she asked, looking him up and down with interest.

"That depends," he replied, "on what you have in mind."

"Well, I was thinking about a room," she said, leaning her elbows on the counter. "After all, this is a hotel."

"That it is," Clint agreed, approaching the desk. Up close he could see that her eyes were brown, her lashes long and graceful. "Well, to tell you the truth, I've already got a room, so what comes after that?"

"You're already checked in?" she asked, looking doubtful.

"That's right," he said. "Just a little while ago. Check it out."

She pulled the register over to do just that, opened it, looked at it briefly, then shut it and pushed it away.

"Clint Adams," she said, thoughtfully. "I know that name from somewhere, don't I?"

"Well, if you do, that puts you one up on me," Clint said, avoiding her question.

"Well, since you are a guest here I guess you're entitled to know," she reasoned. "My name is Dorian Ward."

"I assume you work here, Miss—is it Miss Ward?"

"It's Mrs.," she said, "but my husband has been dead two years now, and I not only work here, I own the place."

"Is that right?"

"Why?" she asked. "Is there something wrong with that?"

"Oh, no, I didn't mean anything like that," he answered. "It's just that you're the prettiest damned hotel owner that I've ever seen."

"Well, you got yourself out of that one pretty well, didn't you?"

"I hope so," he said, grinning. This one was all woman, and a lot of woman, and suddenly the stay in Bear Pass was looking better and better.

"Uh, what kind of bath facilities does your establishment have, Mrs. Ward?"

"Excellent ones, Mr. Adams," she replied. "We've got towels, soap and everything."

"Could you direct me?"

"Certainly," she said. "In fact, I'll take care of you myself—if you don't mind a woman drawing your bath water for you."

"Why, no, I don't mind that at all," he said. "I'll just go on up to my room and grab myself a change of clothes."

"Fine. When you come down just walk along that hallway there and go in the first door on your right. I'll have your bath ready for you."

"Thank you kindly."

"What kind of water do you like, Mr. Adams?" she asked.

"As hot as you can get it, Mrs. Ward . . . and since you are drawing my bath water for me, I think you should call me Clint. After all, that is a pretty intimate thing for a woman to do for a man, isn't it?"

She smiled at him and asked, "Compared to what?"

Clint let that one pass. "I'll get my clean clothes."

"Fine," she said. "I'll be waiting for you."

A man and a woman sometimes need only a few seconds to know that something will happen between them. Clint had been in that situation before, and he'd misread it once or twice, but for the most part he'd been right, and he felt that way now. He felt excited at the prospect of bedding down Dorian Ward, and hoped he wasn't in for a disappointment. After all, all she said was that she was going to draw his bath, and be waiting for him. On the surface, that didn't mean any more than what it said.

He grabbed some clean clothes, and then left to go back downstairs. Looking beyond the bath—and whatever might come with it—he hoped that the Montana House had a decent kitchen. All of a sudden he realized how hungry he was.

Following her instructions, he found his way to the first door on the right. The tub was filled with hot water, and there was a layer of steam lying on the air, hovering near the ceiling.

"I hope it won't be too hot," Dorian Ward said.

He looked to his right and saw her standing there, holding an empty bucket. She bent over to put the bucket down, and he noticed the sheen of perspiration on her forehead, upper lip, and the slopes of her breasts. He could see her breasts because she had opened the first two or three buttons of her shirt.

"Drawing a bath like that is hot work," she said, wiping the back of her hand across her brow.

"I appreciate it," he said.

"Oh, it doesn't come free," she said. "The bath is two bits."

"I think I can handle that." He started to reach into his pocket, but she stopped him.

"You can pay for the bath after," she said.

"All right."

"Let me have your shirt and I'll hang it up for you," she offered.

"Much obliged," he said. He put down his change of clothes, unbuttoned the shirt he was wearing, peeled if off and handed it to her. He expected her to hang it up and then leave—although he was hoping for something different—but she came right back up to him and said, "Now the pants."

She seemed very impersonal about it and he was starting to think that perhaps he *had* read the situation wrong this time. He unbuckled his pants, then took them off and handed them to her. Without giving him a second glance, she walked to the far wall to hang them up.

Beginning to feel embarrassed—and surprised at

himself for it—he quickly removed his underwear while her back was turned and got into the tub, nearly scalding himself in the process. She turned at his sharp intake of breath and asked, "Hot enough for you?"

"It's hot enough," he assured her.

"I'll close the door," she said, walking past him and out of his line of sight. Hearing the door close, he assumed that he was now alone and began to bathe. When he suddenly felt a pair of hands touch his shoulders, he almost reached for his gun, until he heard her voice.

"Would you like me to wash your back?"

"I thought you were gone—" he started to say, but when he turned he was struck dumb by what he saw.

Dorian Ward was totally naked.

Chapter Seven

Dorian Ward's breasts were incredibly firm and round for their size, with large brown areolas and nipples. There were rivulets of perspiration rolling down the valley between her impressive breasts, and Clint found himself following the course of one in particular, which continued on down until it disappeared into her navel.

Clint turned with barely suppressed eagerness, rising to his knees in the tub, and palmed both of those marvelous breasts. He slid his hands to cup the undersides and leaned forward to capture the right nipple between his teeth. His erection was painfully prodding the side of the tub.

Dorian sighed and slid her hands along his shoulders and up his neck until she was holding his head in her hands, pulling him tightly to her breast.

She allowed him to suckle her breasts for a few moments—during which time he also sampled the sweat beads between her breasts, savoring their salty flavor—and then she gathered up two handfuls of his hair and pulled his face away, saying, "Let me get in with you."

He backed away, realizing then that, while there were a couple of other tubs in the room, this was the largest, and now he knew why she'd given it to him.

She lifted one leg over the lip of the tub, exposing the tangled growth of chestnut pubic hair, then brought the other leg over and settled into the hot water, which came to just below her breasts.

"I'll wash your chest," she offered, picking up a wash rag and the soap.

"Do you perform this service for all the guests?" he asked.

"Very few, Mr. Adams," she said. "In fact, to the best of my recollection, you are the first."

"I'm honored," he said.

She moved close to him, sliding her legs along the outside of his, so that she could rub the soap over his chest and shoulders. When he was sufficiently soaped, she began rubbing her hands over his nipples in circular motions, and he picked up the soap and began doing the same thing to her.

As Dorian's hands slid lower, rubbing his belly, the back of her hands began to brush his swollen cock, sending little tremors of pleasure through his loins. He plunged his hands beneath the surface of the water to rub her belly, and then her pubic hair. Suddenly, Dorian grabbed his fleshy pole with both hands, leaned forward and kissed him hard, thrusting her tongue deep into his mouth. At the same time his fingers probed the chestnut forest between her legs until he was able to dip a finger into her honeyed love tunnel. She began to slide up and down the single digit, at the same time fondling his penis with one hand and sliding the other beneath his balls. He slid another finger inside of her and her movements became so frenzied that water began to slosh over the side of the tub.

"Oh, God," she breathed, breaking the kiss, "I

need this,'' and gave his penis a gentle yank.

He withdrew his fingers from her warmth and slid both arms around her so that he could draw her to him. As soon as he entered her he felt his cock begin to throb, and for a moment he thought he was going to shoot into her right there and then, but he made a concerted effort to hold back his orgasm, and succeeded.

Dorian, on the other hand, climaxed as soon as he entered her, and then began to ride up and down his long erection, splashing even more water over the side and onto the floor.

"I'll wash you," she said into his ear, "before we empty the tub."

Still riding his rigid penis, she recaptured the soap and began to wash his back. He cupped her buttocks in his hands and helped her ride him up and down, bracing his heels against the bottom of the tub as best he could. Still soaping his back she kissed him, and he sucked her tongue in and chewed it gently, a favor which she quickly returned.

"Oh, God," she said, suddenly, "I feel it . . . again . . ." and then she was no longer riding him, but bouncing on him, and more than half of the water was now gone from the tub.

As her tremors went on, Clint suddenly relaxed his hold over his own pleasure and allowed himself to begin filling her. The feel of his hot semen seemed to trigger another set of tremors inside of her, and they were both moving around so violently that the tub suddenly tilted to the left, hung there for a second, and then crashed over on its side, spilling the remainder of the water and the two intertwined people to the floor.

● ● ●

When they had successfully disentangled themselves, Clint helped Dorian dry the floor as best they could, and then they dressed and she took him to the dining room for dinner.

"You've sampled my wares, now sample the wares of my kitchen," was the way she put it.

"I can tell you right now," he answered, "that they'll take a poor second."

"Sweet man," she said.

She escorted him to the dining room where she made sure he had a good table and the best meal her kitchen had to offer coming to him. When she frowned at his choice of a table—one from which he would be able to see the entire room—Clint realized with some satisfaction that she had no idea who he was, other than a guest she had just had a very pleasant bath with.

"Enjoy your dinner," she said.

"Not as much as my bath," he assured her, and she smiled, genuinely pleased by his remark.

"You are a sweet man," she said, again.

"Aren't you going to have dinner with me?" he asked, as she made no move to sit down.

"Unfortunately," she replied, "duty calls. Will we have some time to spend together? Are you staying in town long?"

"Three days, at least," he said.

"Well," she said, smiling, "that's a start."

Chapter Eight

True to the Gunsmith's word his meal, although a fine one, could not come close to being as enjoyable as his bath had been. Still, he'd be sure to tell Dorian that he enjoyed it.

When he left the dining room and entered the lobby, the nattily dressed little man was once again behind the counter, and Dorian was nowhere in sight. Instead of asking for her, he decided to let her take care of whatever business it was that she had, and go on over to the saloon for a drink. Maybe he'd even be able to scare up a poker game.

When he entered the saloon the look on the bartender's face reminded him that the man knew who he was, and had passed that information on to Hank Pride.

"A beer," he said when he reached the bar.

"Yes *sir*," the bartender said, and hurriedly fetched it and put it down in front of him. "Nice and cold," the man added, grinning nervously.

"Thanks."

Clint picked up the beer and then turned to survey the room. It was still fairly early in the evening and the saloon was just about half filled. There were no house gambling tables, but there was a poker game going on at a corner table, with a chair open.

Clint settled down at the bar to watch the game and the players and decide if it was the kind of game he would want to sit in on. While he was watching, Sheriff Hanson came in and walked to the bar.

"Buy you a beer, Sheriff?" Clint offered.

"Don't mind if you do," the lawman said. When he had a beer in hand the sheriff looked at Clint and followed his line of sight.

"Are you a poker player?"

"I've been known to sit in on a hand or two," Clint replied.

"You don't want to sit in on that game," Hanson said.

"Why not?" Clint asked, looking at the lawman.

"Strictly amateur stuff," the man replied. "You might win a lot, but you wouldn't enjoy yourself much, and I get the feeling you play more for the enjoyment."

"Is there a better game in town?"

"As a matter of fact, there is," Hanson said. "And there's still time for you to make it."

"Where is it?"

"Out at the Lockman ranch."

"Lockman?"

"Calvin Lockman," Hanson said. "Big man in these parts—the biggest, actually, and he likes to play poker."

Clint thought it over for a moment, then said, "Might be too rich for my blood."

"I doubt it," Hanson said. "The other players are mostly townspeople, and they can't match Lockman's pocket. No, I get the feeling this game might be right up your alley. If you're interested, I can take you out there and make the introductions."

"Do you play?"

"No."

Clint swirled the beer in his glass and thought it over. He came to the decision that he would prefer a more interesting poker game than the one that was going on in the corner, and finally he said, "All right, Sheriff. I'll take you up on your offer—as long as you don't think they'll mind a stranger sitting in."

"I'm sure they won't," the lawman said. "Another hand is always welcome."

"When can we leave?"

"As soon as I clear up some things at my office and let my deputy know where I'll be," Hanson said. He put his beer down, virtually untouched, and said, "I'll come back for you here."

"Fine."

"See you in a few minutes," Hanson said, and left.

When Hanson entered his office he was pleased to find one of his deputies, Dave King, present.

"Dave, I've got a job for you, and it has to be done fast," Hanson said.

King unwound his six-foot-six frame from the chair he was sitting in and asked, "What's up?"

"Round up . . . ." Hanson started to say, then stopped to think a moment before continuing, "—George Armstrong, Joe McDowell, Bob Geary—"

"McDowell's the bank president," King reminded the sheriff.

"I know who he is, damn it!" Hanson said. "Just get him, and the rest."

"What do I tell them?"

"Tell them to get out to Lockman's place fast."

"What for?"

"A poker game."

"A poker—"

"And grab anyone else you can think of to fill out a table," Hanson went on. "Then ride out there with them and tell Lockman that he's having his regular poker game tonight."

Frowning, King said, "Sheriff, as far as I know, Lockman don't have a regular poker game."

"Well," Hanson said, "tell him he does now."

"*Tell* Lockman—" King started to say in surprise.

"And tell him that I'm bringing Clint Adams out in a little while to play," Hanson added.

"Adams?" the deputy asked. "The Gunsmith? He's in Bear Pass? Since—"

"Dave!" Hanson said, cutting the man off. "Just go and do it, huh? Now!"

"Yes sir," the deputy said.

When the deputy left, Hanson sat down behind his desk to stall for time, shuffling papers just in case Clint Adams got impatient and came over to see what was taking him so long.

Suddenly Hanson stopped as a thought struck him, and he wondered if Calvin Lockman even knew how to play poker.

"Ready to go?" Hanson asked Clint, returning to the saloon.

As Hanson had entered, Clint had been in the process of ordering another beer. Now he turned to the bartender and said, "Cancel that beer," then turned to the lawman and said, "I'm more than ready, Sheriff."

"I'm sorry I took so long," Hanson said, "but there was more to take care of than I thought."

"Are you sure it's not too late to go out there?"

"Don't worry about that," Hanson said. "I just

hope you don't mind if the game goes on late.''

''*I* don't mind if *they* don't,'' Clint replied. ''The longer it goes on, the more I stand to win.''

''Or lose.''

''I don't lose,'' Clint said.

''You're pretty confident,'' Hanson said as they left the saloon together and headed for the livery.

''That's the only attitude to have when you're playing poker,'' Clint explained.

''I suppose you're right,'' Hanson said.

''Oh, that's right,'' Clint said. ''You said before you don't gamble.''

''No,'' Hanson said, touching the Gunsmith's arm, ''I didn't say that. What I said was, I don't play poker. I never said I don't gamble.''

''I'm sorry,'' Clint said. ''I guess I must have misunderstood.''

Chapter Nine

Clint was puzzled by the leisurely pace Hanson seemed to be setting on the way to the Lockman ranch. Once or twice he tried to pick it up, but Hanson made the same remark each time about needing to buy himself a new horse, and Clint slowed Duke down to match Hanson's pace. By the time they reached Lockman's ranch, he was convinced that something more than a poker game was in store for him, and he was curious to find out what it was.

"Nice place," he commented as they stopped in front of Lockman's house.

"It's the biggest house and spread in the country," Hanson said.

"I don't doubt it," Clint said, dismounting.

"Hang on and I'll get someone to take care of the horses," Hanson said.

Clint started to protest, but Hanson bounded up the steps and entered the house as if he belonged there. A few moments went by, and then the lawman reappeared with another man.

"Jed here will take the horses to the barn," he said. "Take extra good care of that big black, Jed. That's prime horse flesh."

"Sure, Sheriff," the man answered. He took the

reins of both horses and started leading them to the barn.

"We can go in now," the sheriff said to Clint.

"All clear, eh?" Clint remarked.

"What?"

"Never mind. Let's go."

Clint followed Hanson up the steps and into the house. The entrance hall was massive, reminding Clint of the house where he had played poker in a town called Two Queens, Nevada.* He hoped that things would not turn out the way they had in Nevada.

"This way," Hanson said, turning to his right. "They're right in here."

Hanson gripped the handles on twin doors and pushed them open, revealing a large round table with five men sitting at it.

"Mr. Adams," one of the men said. "Glad you could join us—aren't we, gentlemen?"

The other men nodded or voiced their assent, but Clint could see that in no case was it wholehearted.

"Mr. Lockman, I presume?" he said.

"You presume correctly," Lockman said, without rising. "Please take a seat and we'll get started."

"You haven't started yet?" Clint asked.

"Uh, well, of course we have," Lockman said, quickly, "but now that you're here, we can get started in earnest. I mean, six does make a better game than five, doesn't it?"

"That depends," Clint said, taking the only empty seat at the table. Luckily, it was facing the room, with a wall at his back, so he did not have to try and get someone to trade seats with him.

---

*The Gunsmith #13: Draw to an Inside Death

"I'll leave you gents to your game," Sheriff Hanson said.

"Don't worry about Mr. Adams," Lockman said. "I'll put him up here for the night, and he can return to town in the morning."

"That's very kind, but—" Clint started to protest, but Lockman gave him no chance.

"No trouble at all," Lockman assured him. "He's in good hands, Sheriff, rest assured."

" 'Night, gents," Hanson said. "Enjoy your game."

Hanson left and shut the doors behind him, and Clint looked at the faces around the table. None of them looked very happy about being there—in fact, some of them looked pretty sleepy, as if they had just woken up . . . and they played that way.

After a few hours, when Clint had an impressive stack of chips in front of him, he knew for sure that poker was not the reason he had been brought out there. A couple of people at the table didn't even appear to have a working knowledge of the finer points of the game—such as a flush beating a straight!

The other players were introduced to Clint, but he made no conscious attempt to remember their names. He was sure that they were inconsequential to whatever it was that was really going on. Lockman was the man he concentrated on. It was supposed to be his poker game, and he appeared to have nothing more than a working knowledge of the game.

After a few hours a couple of the men actually appeared to be dozing off, and Clint decided to help them out.

"It's getting kind of late, isn't it?" he asked.

A man named McDowell—who Clint had figured out was the bank manager—looked up, quickly opening his eyes, and said, "Yes, it is, isn't it?"

Lockman gave the man a dirty look but, undaunted, McDowell said, "I do have a bank to open in the morning."

"We all have businesses to open in the morning," said a man Clint thought he remembered had been introduced as George Armstrong.

"It seems that I'm the big winner," Clint said, "but I have no objection to the game breaking up early if the rest of you don't."

Now when the men at the table nodded their assent, it was wholeheartedly. Even Lockman finally agreed and looked relieved.

While the others rose to leave, hastily donning their jackets, Clint stayed in his seat, watching Lockman.

"Even though we're breaking up earlier than expected," Lockman said, "you're still welcome to spend the night."

"I think I'll spend just enough time to find out why you really had me brought out here . . . maybe over a drink of something expensive?"

As the others filed out without a word to their host, Lockman said, "I guess we didn't fool you, huh?"

"I feel so guilty I may give all this money back," Clint said.

"Forget it. I can afford it, and so can they. Let's go into the other room and have some brandy, and I'll explain."

"Sure. I might as well, since I'm already here."

He stood up, gathered up his winnings and followed Calvin Lockman through a doorway into another room. It was full of plush, expensive furniture, and in one corner was a long, well-stocked bar that put the one in the saloon to shame.

"What'll it be?" Lockman asked, slipping behind the bar. It was obvious that the man enjoyed playing bartender.

"How about some of that brandy you mentioned?" Clint asked.

"You've got it. Come on, belly up."

Clint moved to the bar and watched Lockman pour him a drink from a crystal decanter.

"There you go," he said, setting a huge snifter in front of him. "Can I get you anything else?"

"Just give me an explanation, Mr. Lockman," Clint said.

"An explanation," Lockman said. "All right, coming up."

Lockman was tall, dark-haired and slick looking, like a gambler—and although he was obviously not a poker player, he had to be a gambler to build up a fortune like the one he obviously had. Clint didn't like his attitude, though. It was too phony. He was buttering the Gunsmith up for something, and stepping out of character to do it.

"Mr. Lockman—"

"Call me Calvin," Lockman said. "Please."

"If you don't mind," Clint said, "I'll call you Mr. Lockman."

Lockman frowned and said, "I don't understand."

"I just want to know what's going on," Clint said, "and I'd appreciate it if you'd tell it to me straight, without the games, or the good host act."

Lockman's face changed then, and Clint knew that he was looking at the real man now, the Calvin

Lockman who had built up a great fortune by being something other than a good host.

"Straight to business, then," Lockman said.

"Right."

"I suppose you've been in town long enough to hear about a bear, a grizzly that's been killing beef in the area."

"And people."

"Yes, and people," Lockman said.

"Ol' Three-Paw."

"That's right," Lockman said. "You have heard of him."

"I've seen him," Clint said. He sipped the brandy and it went down nice and smooth . . . and expensive.

"You saw him," Lockman said. "That's right. That's what Sheriff Hanson told me. You saw him close to town."

"So?"

"I know your reputation, Mr. Adams," Lockman said. "I know you used to be a lawman, and that means that you've hunted in your time."

"Men," Clint said, "not bears."

"How different could it be?" Lockman asked.

"Have you ever hunted?"

Lockman frowned and said, "No, but—"

"That makes us even, then, because I've never made a fortune. Where we're not even, though, is that I would never try and tell you how easy it was to make your fortune, so you shouldn't try and tell me how easy or hard it is to hunt."

"All right," Lockman said, "you've made your point. Let me put it another way. I would like to pay you a substantial amount of money to hunt down and kill Ol' Three-Paw."

"I see," Clint said. "Would this substantial amount of money be coming from the town, the ranchers . . . or from just you?"

"Well, since this animal is killing beef, and I own most of the beef in these parts, I'm putting up the reward."

"Reward?"

"Yes. When tomorrow's paper hits the street, it will have an offer of a reward to anyone who can kill Ol' Three-Paw. In addition, I have posters circulating with the same offer."

"So I'd be hunting the grizzly for the reward?"

"No, our arrangement would be separate."

"How much of a reward are you offering?"

"Five thousand dollars."

"That's going to bring a lot of people to Bear Pass," Clint said.

"Probably."

"A lot of them will be amateurs, shooting at anything that moves," Clint went on.

"I've been told that," Lockman said.

"How do you feel about that?"

"I'll do anything to get this grizzly, Adams," Lockman said. "He can turn Bear Pass into a ghost town. If one of those amateurs happened to get him, it would be worth the trouble others might cause."

"This grizzly is more likely to get them, Lockman," Clint said. "You're turning this area into a shooting gallery."

"I want that bear."

Clint finished his brandy and put the glass down on the bar. "How much are you offering me?"

"Twice the amount of the reward."

"That's a substantial amount, all right," Clint agreed.

"Will you do it?"

"I don't know, Mr. Lockman," Clint said. "I'll have to think about it."

"Don't think too long, Clint," Lockman said, "or somebody else might bag this beast."

"Sure," Clint said. He knew that if Lockman really thought that someone else had a chance to kill Ol' Three-Paw, he wouldn't be offering the Gunsmith ten thousand dollars to hunt the creature down. "I'll let you know tomorrow, Mr. Lockman."

"Of course," Lockman said, "you want to sleep on it. I'll have someone show you to your room—"

"That won't be necessary," Clint assured him. "I can find my way back to town."

"You could stay here overnight without having to feel any sort of obligation," Lockman said.

"Yes," Clint said, "I could—but I won't. Good night, Mr. Lockman."

Chapter Ten

"Well, you keep late hours for a stranger," Dorian Ward commented.

Clint turned his head from the door to his room and saw Dorian standing down the hall, in the doorway of what was apparently her own room. She was wearing a white, floor-length nighgown, and the light from her room was turning the diaphanous material virtually invisible. She was a breathtaking sight.

"What could you have found to do?" she wondered aloud.

"A poker game," he said. "You weren't worried, were you? Maybe waiting up for me?"

"I like to look out for my guests," she replied. "Especially those who don't know their way around town yet."

"I see. What did you have in mind to show me tonight?"

"Well," she said, drumming her fingers on the elbows of her folded arms, "we could start with my room. It has the best bed in town."

"Well," he said, turning away from his door, "that sounds like an offer I can't refuse."

"I thought it might," she said, and walked into her room. Clint walked down the hall and followed her in.

The diaphanous gown had now disappeared, and she stood by her bed totally nude. Her large, full breasts were thrust out towards him, their nipples already hardened with desire.

He removed his clothing under her watchful eye, and then they fell to her bed clasped together. Clint had a moment to realize that her mattress was indeed a superior one before she was suddenly atop him, already impaled on his long, hard shaft.

"I've been waiting for this ever since our bath," she said. "We didn't quite finish what we started then."

"The bathtub didn't exactly cooperate with us, if you remember," he told her.

"Well, this bed won't fall over," she assured him, and then she set to bouncing up and down on him, as if she were trying to make a liar out of herself.

Clint reached around to cup her impressive buttocks, and sought to use his strength to control her tempo. She fought him for a few moments, but then gave in and began to ride him in deep, even strokes. Every time the tip of his penis bumped into her core she caught her breath and then let it out in a rush. He lifted his head to tongue her nipples, and as soon as he sucked one into his mouth her entire body seemed to start quivering. Her pussy sucked at him furiously as her spasms continued, but he was not yet ready to let himself go.

"Oh, God," she said, when her spasms of pleasure had subsided. "You didn't—"

"Not yet," he said, turning her over, "but I will . . . in time!"

Kneeling astride her he began to devour her nipples and breasts, biting the firm mounds of flesh, and chewing the large, nugget-sized nipples. Eventually he worked his way down over her belly, pausing to tongue her deep navel, and then moving lower and delving even deeper. As his tongue entered her moist, sweetened cleft she caught his head between her thighs and tangled her fingers in his hair.

As his tongue ignited a raging fire in her loins she arched her back and pumped her hips in time to his oral thrusts, and just when she had started to think that nothing could ever feel as good as this, his tongue moved up and began to circle her engorged love-bud. Suddenly her hips were pumping in a frenzied tempo of her own and he had to forcefully pin her to the bed in order to continue manipulating her.

"Oh, yes, hold me down, hold me down," she cried out. "Suck me, suck it, please, please . . ."

He pursed his lips around her rigid clit and began to suck, and then flick it with his tongue, and then suck again.

"That's it, that's it," she cried, and then her belly trembled like the ground during an earthquake, and she exploded. . . .

"Oh, God!" she cried, and he swiftly raised himself above her and speared her with his cock, right in the midst of her orgasm. Her cry this time was soundless and she wrapped her powerful legs around his hips and raked his back with her nails as he drove into her again and again, until finally his seed virtually burst from him, filling her with a million little burning needles. . . .

"You played poker with who?" she asked later, as he explained where he had been so late at night.

"With Calvin Lockman."

"I didn't know Calvin played poker."

"He doesn't," Clint said, "and neither do any of the other men who were at the game."

"I don't understand," she said. "If that's the case, then what were you doing there?"

"The sheriff and Lockman worked it out between them just to get me out there."

"What for?"

"Lockman wanted to offer me a job."

"Doing what?"

"Hunting down Ol' Three-Paw."

"*What?*" she asked. "Why you?"

He hesitated a moment, then said, "I have something of a reputation, Dorian."

"As a hunter?"

"As an ex-lawman," he said, "and with a gun."

"So," she said, showing no surprise at all, although he was still certain she had no idea who he really was, "because you can handle a gun pretty well he wants you to go after that monster?"

"That's it."

"And what did you tell him?"

"I told him I'd think about it."

"Well, think about it and then tell him no," she advised.

"Why?"

"That animal is more than just a bear, Clint," she said. "A lot of people around here talk about it as if it were something . . . supernatural."

"That's silly," he said. "It's just a bear—bigger than most, maybe, but still an animal."

"Have you ever hunted an animal down before?" she asked.

"I've shot my share of wolves and wildcats," he said.

"I mean something this large, this mean."

"Not exactly," he said, and suddenly he thought of the Sasquatch, the fabled Big Foot, and wondered why he hadn't equated the two before.

"What does that mean?"

"It means," he said, thoughtfully, "that I may just have made up my mind."

Thinking of the Sasquatch also made him think of the big Parker-Hale, a big game rifle he had gotten from an Englishman named Wardell, with which to hunt Big Foot.* That rifle had punched a mighty big hole in the Sasquatch, and might be just the thing to bring down Ol' Three-Paw.

"You're going to do it, aren't you?"

"Well, he is offering a lot of money," he reasoned, "and the reward he's offering is going to get a lot of innocent people hurt or killed. If I can bring down that grizzly, it might save a lot of trouble."

"And it might get you killed," she added, but by then he wasn't listening to her, and she knew it would be useless to go on arguing. She knew the look on a man's face when he's made up his mind to do something, and there was very little a woman could do to change it.

Being married had at least taught her that.

---

*The Gunsmith #21: Sasquatch Hunt

Chapter Eleven

Early the next morning Clint left the hotel and went over to the livery. The rear wheels and axle had been removed from his rig, and it was propped up on two kegs.

"Hank!" he called out.

Big Hank Pride came out from the back and grinned when he saw the Gunsmith.

"I ain't got that axle yet," he said, apologetically.

"I know that," Clint assured him. "I didn't expect you to. I just want to know if I can climb in the back of my rig."

Hank shrugged and said, "As long as you don't start jumping around while you're in there."

"I'll try to contain myself," Clint promised.

Hank laughed and returned to his work, and Clint climbed inside his rig.

He found what he was looking for very easily. A gun the size of the Parker-Hale was hard to misplace. It had two massive barrels of beautifully blued metal, a hand-carved rosewood stock, and was a larger weapon overall than even the Big Fifty Sharps buffalo gun. At sixty caliber it was, in fact, more powerful than the Sharps, and would not only drop a charging buffalo, but an elephant, as well.

This was the weapon he would use if he went hunting for Ol' Three-Paw.

Fondling the gun in his hands, the Gunsmith thought back to the only time he'd ever used it, against the Sasquatch. He had hit the creature once and although the single shot did not kill him, he was sure that one more would have. Unfortunately, at the time, he had not had any additional ammunition for the weapon, and had since measured and loaded his own—not that he had ever expected to need the gun again, but it never hurt to be ready.

The Parker-Hale had an effective range of over nine hundred yards, with tremendous knockdown force, and that was just what Clint knew he would need against Ol' Three-Paw.

Clint left the rig with the Parker-Hale and ammunition, and Hank, coming out from the back again, stopped short when he saw the massive weapon in the Gunsmith's hands.

"Jesus, I ain't never seen a gun that big before."

"It's a big-game rifle," Clint explained.

"What kind of game could be that big?" Hank asked—then raised his eyebrows as he realized just what kind of game *was* that big.

"You going after Ol' Three-Paw?"

"I'm thinking about it."

"You don't need no kind of gun to think about it," Hank said, "but with that kind of gun, I'd say you pretty much made up your mind already."

"Yeah, well, maybe I have," Clint said.

"Well, if you decide for sure that you are, make sure you let me know."

"Why?" Clint asked. "You want to cancel your order on that axle?"

"No," Hank said. "If you go after that grizzly, you're gonna need somebody to back you up."

Clint was immediately sorry for his remark and said, "I appreciate that, Hank, I really do."

"Sure," Hank said, wiping his hands on a rag. "I got to get back to work now, but remember what I said."

"I'll remember," Clint promised. As the big man turned and shambled to the back of the livery Clint said in a lower voice, "You can bet on it."

Chapter Twelve

Clint took the Parker-Hale to his room, cleaned it, then went downstairs to have breakfast, leaving the gun behind. There was little chance he'd be needing it in the hotel dining room.

When he was brought a newspaper with his coffee he knew that although he had not seen Dorian that morning—since leaving her room, that is—she had obviously seen him.

Drinking his coffee and waiting for his breakfast, he read Calvin Lockman's announcement of the reward of five thousand dollars for anyone who could kill Ol' Three-Paw and prove it. What did he expect them to do, he wondered, load the carcass onto the back of a mule and bring it to him?

When his breakfast came he folded the newspaper so that he could see the boxed announcement, and studied it while he ate.

In spite of what Hank Pride had said, Clint had still not completely made up his mind about hunting the grizzly. For one thing, he did not like Calvin Lockman, although he could think of no good reason why. It must have been instinct, and Clint Adams had come to trust his instincts without reservation over the years. For another thing, he did not like the idea of the reward. Even less did he like the idea of hunting for Ol' Three-

Paw with a bunch of amateurs with guns running around loose.

Still, there was curiosity, and there was the challenge, the new excitement. Those had been some of the reasons he'd gone looking for the Sasquatch, and he had been lucky to escape that time with his life.

It had been exciting, though, there could be no denying that.

"Still trying to decide?" Dorian Ward asked. He looked up to find her standing by his table with her hands on her hips, and she added, "I'd like to think that I had something to do with any second thoughts you're having."

"You have second thoughts after you've made a decision. The only decision I've made is to ask you to have a cup of coffee with me, and I have no second thoughts about that."

"Or about last night, I hope," she said, sitting across from him.

"About last night," he replied, "I'm having second, third and fourth thoughts, and they're all good."

"Sweet talk me all you want," she said, "but tell me you're not going after that grizzly."

"I'm tempted."

"To what? Tell me, or go?"

"Both."

"You can't have it both ways," she argued. "Either you want to commit suicide, or you don't."

"That's not fair."

"Maybe not," she said, but offered no apology.

She remained quiet while Clint poured her a cup of coffee, then said, "I did some checking on you."

"Is that so?"

"Yes," she said. "I went to the newspaper and read

some very interesting old clips.''

"Did you like what you read?''

"Not really, but then I don't believe everything I read, either,'' she said. She sipped her coffee and there was another awkward silence between them.

"Does this urge to go after a bear have anything to do with your reputation?'' she finally asked.

"You mean, am I trying to add to it?''

"I don't know what I mean,'' she replied. "I'm just trying to understand.''

"Don't try,'' he suggested, "because I don't quite understand it, either.''

"That makes a lot of sense.''

"I didn't say it did.''

"I have to leave,'' she said, standing up.

"Business?'' he asked.

"You're making me feel frustrated and angry,'' she said, "and I don't want to cause a scene here in my own place.''

"Fine,'' he said.

"We can talk later,'' she said, and then added, "if you like.''

"Sure,'' he said.

She hesitated a moment, apparently waiting for him to say something else, but when nothing else was forthcoming she walked away.

Dorian Ward was an additional problem that Clint Adams didn't need. She was pleasant to be with, there was no doubt about that, and it would be difficult to avoid her in her own hotel, but if she didn't stop trying to influence his decisions, that was just what he was going to have to try and do.

He hoped it wouldn't come to that.

Chapter Thirteen

Clint decided to take the day before giving his reply to Calvin Lockman and talking to anyone in town who had seen—or claimed to have seen—Ol' Three-Paw.

He started at the saloon, talking to the bartender. If anyone had a story to tell about the big grizzly, the bartender certainly would have been among the first to hear about it.

"So," the bartender said, placing a beer in front of Clint, "you want to know who's seen Ol' Three-Paw."

"That's right."

"Interested in the reward, huh?"

"Not really," Clint said. "I've seen the grizzly myself; I'm just interested in who else has seen him."

"A lot of people claim to have seen him," the man said, giving Clint a look that said he might be among them, "but the problem is, who do you believe?"

"You been a bartender long?" Clint asked.

The man, who was in his late forties, drew himself up straight and said, "For twenty years or so."

"Then don't tell me that you have trouble telling the truth from a tall tale."

The bartender grinned, showing bad teeth, and said, "You're right about that. I can usually tell."

"Then tell me."

"Well," the man said, rubbing his jaw and milking

57

his moment in the sun, "there have been a few fellas claiming to have seen Ol' Three-Paw, but only one that I ever believed."

"Who's that?"

"A breed name of Dusty," the bartender said.

"A half-breed?"

"That's right."

"Where do I find him?"

"Out there," the bartender answered, waving a hand in the general direction of the hills. "He comes in every so often for supplies, but most of the time he just stays out there, where Ol' Three-Paw lives."

"What's his story?"

"I don't think anybody knows that," the man answered. "I don't even know what kind of Indian blood he's got, or whether it came from his ma or pa."

"Does he drink here?"

"Don't serve no Indians," the bartender said, standing up straight again. "Never have and never will, not even a half-breed."

"I see."

"So if you want to know about Ol' Three-Paw, you'll have to go out there and find Dusty," the barkeep said, then added, "Only you best be careful you don't find Ol' Three-Paw himself, first."

"There's nobody else you can think of?"

"Well," the bartender said, "you might want to talk to Dorian Ward over at the Montana House."

"Dorian Ward?" Clint asked, showing his surprise. "She's seen Ol' Three-Paw?"

"Well, you better talk to her about that," the other man said. "You see, her husband was killed by a bear up Montana way some years back, and I've heard that she claims that it was the same bear."

Chapter Fourteen

"You said you'd be available to talk," Clint said when Dorian Ward answered her door.

"Come in," she said, stepping back. When he was inside she closed the door, turned and leaned against it. "Have you made up your mind?"

"Tell me about your husband," he said, ignoring her question.

Her temper flared and she said, "You don't have any right to ask that."

"Of course I do," he replied. "If I'm going out after that bear, then I should know everything there is to know about him. If you have any information about him, I have a right to know."

"Then you *are* going after him!"

"If what I heard is true, you should be glad I'm going," he said. "I'd think that you'd want to go, too—not that I'd allow you to."

Her shoulders slumped as she said, "I don't want to go, I don't want you to go, I don't want anyone to go. I don't want anyone else to die, not the way my husband did."

"Tell me about it, please," Clint asked, quietly.

She nodded, and moved to sit down on the bed. He pulled a chair away from the window and sat opposite her.

"It was in Billings, Montana," she said in a low voice. "We had a hotel there, a successful business, and we were happy—and then he came."

"Who?"

"That . . . that creature," she said, with the hatred showing plainly on her face. "He began to terrorize the ranchers in the area, just as he's doing here, and Henry—my husband, Henry Ward—was afraid that Billings would become a ghost town, and we would lose everything we had. He decided to go after the bear, and kill it."

"But it killed him?"

"There's more to it than that," she said, shaking her head. "It killed him in more ways than one."

She paused, and Clint allowed her to tell it all in her own good time.

"He became obsessed with killing that bear. He neglected the business, his health . . . and our marriage. He'd go out hunting, stayed away days, sometimes weeks, and then come back for supplies and go right out again."

Again she paused, and he waited patiently.

"He'd been gone for weeks when they brought him in," she said, finally breaking the silence. "He was all clawed, bleeding, and all he could talk about was how big the bear was, and that he'd gotten a shot off at him just before he jumped him. He was proud of that . . . and he died for it."

She paused again, then said, "Stupid. Stupid men!"

"Dorian," Clint said, speaking softly, "tell me why you think it's the same bear."

She was fighting back tears, and doing it successfully, determined not to cry for a man who had died of his own stupidity almost two years before.

"Henry was right when he said that he'd shot the bear, but all he had done was crease him on the right shoulder. Some people who saw the bear after that incident said that the crease had healed, but that the hair had grown back in gray."

"Does Ol' Three-Paw have a gray streak on his right shoulder?" Clint asked.

"I don't know," she said "I haven't see him since—"

"Since what?" he prompted.

"Since I left Montana and came here to get away from him," she finished.

"People in town think you were heading for Montana when you settled here."

"That's what I told them."

"Why?"

She hesitated, then explained in a rush of words barely understandable. "Because I knew he'd follow me here, and I didn't want to be blamed."

"For what?"

"For bringing that bear here, to do what he did in Billings."

"Dorian, do you seriously believe that this bear has followed you here from Montana?"

"Yes!" she hissed, "Yes, yes, yes! To kill me, the same way he killed Henry!"

"Dorian—" he began, reaching out for her, but she cringed from his touch.

"Please, Clint," she said, hugging herself as if she were cold, "I'd rather you left now. Please."

"All right."

He got up and walked toward the door, and she spoke to him once more.

"Please, think about what I've told you," she said.

"Don't go after that bear."

He didn't answer, because suddenly he was sure that he *was* going after that bear—even if it was just to find out if the beast had a gray streak on its left shoulder!

Chapter Fifteen

Clint was having dinner in the hotel dining room when Sheriff Hanson approached him.

"Mind if I sit down?" Hanson asked.

"Long as you don't expect me to share," Clint replied. "Except for the coffee, that is."

"Coffee's fine," the sheriff said.

"Help yourself, then," Clint said, indicating the pot and a second cup with a stab of his fork.

The sheriff sat down and poured himself a cup of coffee.

"What's on your mind, Sheriff?"

"Calvin Lockman was wondering what you decided about his offer," Hanson answered.

"You run errands for Lockman?"

The question failed to insult Hanson. "He's an important man in these parts, with a big future."

"You going to be part of that future?"

"You never know."

"You're an ambitious man, then."

"There are worse things to be," Hanson said. Clint looked at him sharply, but apparently there was no insult intended.

"Well?" Hanson said.

"Well what?"

"What did you decide?"

The Gunsmith carefully chewed a mouthful of steak and potatoes before answering. "Tell him I'll give it a shot."

Hanson smiled and said, "He'll be glad to hear that."

"Tell him I still don't like the idea of the reward, though," Clint added. "It's going to make my job much harder."

"He wouldn't be paying you as much if it was easy," Hanson replied.

"I guess that's true."

Hanson took a sip of his coffee, made a face at how strong it was and put it down. "I guess I'll give him your answer, then."

"You do that," Clint said. "And tell him one other thing."

"What's that?" Hanson asked, rising.

"Tell him I'll be taking along a backup, and I expect my man to be paid well."

"Not as well as you, I hope."

"No," Clint agreed, "not quite that well, but well enough."

"I'll tell him."

"I'll wait for his answer," Clint said. "My backup is a condition of the job. Make sure he understands that."

"He will," Hanson assured him. "He never lays out that kind of money without fully understanding what he's paying for."

"That's good," Clint said. "I want us each to know where we stand."

"I'll tell him," Hanson said. "Thanks for the coffee."

"My pleasure."

Clint watched the lawman's retreating back until it disappeared into the lobby, then put his fork down and turned his attention to the pot of strong coffee. Hank Pride would be glad to know that he had a job that would pay him more than he could otherwise earn in a year.

Now all Clint had to find out was if the man could handle a gun.

Chapter Sixteen

Lacy Blake made her living hunting—men.

Ever since a group of men had killed her mother and two sisters when she was sixteen years old she had been hunting, both for vengeance and for a living.

There had been five men at their ranch that day ten years ago, and over the years she had found and killed three of them. Only two remained, and she knew that one day their paths would cross, and she would kill them as well.

After ten years of hunting, she had become proficient with both handgun and rifle, as well as becoming a near expert tracker.

She was in Wyoming when she read the article in the paper offering five thousand dollars reward for killing a grizzly. Five thousand dollars would carry her a long way in her quest for those remaining two men.

"Five thousand for a bear," she said to her partner, handing him the paper.

Jake Benteen accepted the paper from her and scanned the piece about the bear. "Ol' Three-Paw," he said, putting the paper down. "I think I've heard something about this grizzly."

"Like what?"

"Like he kills people."

"Probably to survive," she said. "Men kill for a lot less."

"And women?" Benteen asked.

"For a lot more," she said.

Lacy Blake had filled out since she was sixteen, and even then she had been beautiful. Now she was breathtaking, with shoulder-length red hair, green sparkling eyes that turned ice cold when she was working, and a full, womanly figure that incited men's minds to thoughts of lazy days and long nights in bed.

Jake Benteen was five years older than Lacy, and a couple of inches shorter. They had been riding together for two years now, and complemented each other perfectly when they were working. When they weren't working, however, they were hard put to even get along, as each had a strong will and mind of their own.

Benteen had been hunting men for a living since he was eighteen, and he had a reputation for doing it well. In the two years they had been riding together, Lacy had learned a lot from him—but would never admit it. To date, their relationship had been strictly business and would probably always remain so.

"Now you want to go after a bear?" he asked her.

"I'm thinking about it," she admitted. "Five thousand dollars is a lot to turn away from."

"Maybe."

"You don't have to come," she said. "We ain't joined at the hip."

"I know that," he said. They had split up before to work on their own, only to join up again later.

"The money's mine if I get him," she said.

"I know that too," Benteen said.

Lacy uncorked the whiskey bottle on the table between them and poured them each a shot.

"How far is that town from here?" she asked Benteen.

He glanced at the article again, even though she knew he remembered every word, and said, "Bear Pass? Probably less than a day's ride—maybe half a day, due north."

"Half a day on Clicker," she said. Clicker was the big bay mare she'd been riding for the past four years, and the best mount she'd ever had. The animal had more speed and stamina than any horse she had ever come across.

"You're probably right."

Benteen did not name his horses, and he changed them fairly often—especially when he had a pocketful of money. Never name something you might one day have to eat, he'd told Lacy a long time ago, but she could never even entertain the idea of being so desperate that she would eat Clicker.

"If I go with you," he said, "my roan would just slow you down. You want to get there before the rush, don't you?"

"Sure."

She finished her drink and then got to her feet. Heads turned in the saloon, and admiring eyes ran over her tall, full figure.

She started to walk out, then stopped short and asked over her shoulder, "Where should we meet?"

He shrugged. "I might be in New Mexico in a couple of weeks, give or take a day."

She nodded, and walked out. She didn't have to ask where in New Mexico. When Jake Benteen got tired, he always went to the same sleepy little town, just to get away from the hunting and killing for a while.

She knew just where she'd find Jake Benteen—after she got that big grizzly and the five thousand dollars that went with it.

Chapter Seventeen

Clint sat in a chair on the boardwalk in front of the hotel and watched the hunters ride into town. It hadn't taken long for the news to circulate, and already they were starting to arrive. Some of them passed by him and entered the hotel to ask after accommodations, and very few of them looked worth the ink it would take to register them.

"Looks like a crowd is starting to gather," someone said.

Clint looked up and saw a tall drink of water with a star pinned to his chest. The deputy was one of the tallest men he'd ever seen, and looked like he didn't have an ounce of meat on him.

"You talking to me?" he asked.

"Yes sir," the deputy said. "My name's Dave King. I'm Sheriff Hanson's deputy."

"I figured that."

"Looks like that reward has starting drawing them in already," the deputy said, "and the offer ain't even a day old yet."

"Looks like," Clint agreed.

The deputy kept talking, trying to make conversation, but at that point Clint's attention was attracted elsewhere.

The woman riding into town was sitting straight and tall, breasts thrust out in front of her impressively. She had long red hair that shone in the sunlight, and she rode the big bay mare with a cool confidence Clint had not seen in many men, let alone a woman.

"Wonder who she is?" King said.

"You're a lawman, Dave," Clint said. "You could easily find out."

"Yeah," King said, "I guess I could."

They both watched her ride to the livery, where she gave her horse over to Hank Pride to be cared for, and then started walking back towards the hotel.

She walked just the way she rode, as if she wasn't afraid of anyone or anything that might stand in her path. She wore a Colt .45 on her hip, and Clint noticed that her hands looked large enough and strong enough to handle the heavy weapon.

As she mounted the boardwalk to walk past him into the hotel their eyes met, and hers did not waver once. They were green, he noticed, and devoid of expression, and he was very curious as to who this woman was, and why she was in town—if it wasn't to hunt for Ol' Three-Paw. The rifle she was carrying in her right hand was a perfectly good Henry, but not the type of weapon you'd expect to be able to take a grizzly down with—unless you nailed him right between the eyes.

Still, he got the distinct impression that if she wanted to, she could.

"Where's the sheriff, Deputy?" he asked.

"I think he went out to Mr. Lockman's place," King replied.

"Then I guess it's up to you to check out the strangers in town, huh?"

"All of 'em?" King asked. "They're probably all here for the reward."

"Well, then, maybe you ought to just check out the more interesting ones," Clint suggested.

"Interesting?" King asked—and then when it dawned on him what Clint meant he grinned and said, "Oh yeah. I get it. Excuse me. I got to check something out."

"Sure," Clint said. "Do your job, Deputy—and let me know if I can help in any way while the sheriff's out of town."

"I'll do that, Mr. Adams."

"Call me Clint, Dave," Clint replied.

"See you later . . . Clint," King said, obviously pleased that he was suddenly on a first-name basis with the legendary Gunsmith.

After the deputy had gone into the hotel, Clint got up and walked over to the livery. He found Hank Pride rubbing down the redhead's mare.

"That's a pretty animal," Clint said, inspecting the horse.

"It sure is," Hank said. "Oh, not as pretty as your Duke, but a nice piece of horseflesh."

"Also not as pretty as the lady who rode in on her," Clint said, patting the mare's nose.

"I'll say," Hank replied, eyes lighting up. "That has to be the prettiest woman I ever laid eyes on."

"I'd have to agree with that," Clint said, rubbing the animal's neck. "Did she say what her name was?"

"The horse?"

"The lady."

"No in either case," Hank said. "She asked me to take special care of her, and paid me in advance—and extra."

"Mmm," Clint said, thoughtfully. "That reminds me, Hank."

"What?"

"Better get somebody to run the livery for you for a while."

"For how long?" Hank asked, stopping his brushing to face Clint.

"I don't know," Clint replied. "That depends on how long it takes us to bring down Ol' Three-Paw."

"All right!" Hank said, and he continued to brush the mare with increased vigor, eyes shining now for a totally different reason than they had been moments before.

Returning to the hotel, Clint saw Sheriff Hanson riding back into town, and stopped in the middle of the street to talk to him.

"Mr. Adams," Hanson said, reining in. "I've just come from Mr. Lockman's place."

"So I gathered."

"Your conditions have been met," the lawman said. "Mr. Lockman will pay your backup whatever you say. He trusts that whatever figure you come up with will be fair."

"I'll try and be worthy of that trust," Clint said. "What about you, Sheriff?" he asked. "Any chance you'll go after that five thousand dollar reward yourself?"

Shaking his head Hanson said, "Not a chance, Adams. I've got other ways to get ahead."

"Yeah," Clint said, "I'll just bet you do."

"When will you be going out after the bear?" Hanson asked.

"I'll have to stock up on supplies, buy a pack animal, and outfit my backup. I'll let Lockman know when I'm ready to leave.''

"I hope it isn't too long."

"It won't be," Clint said. "I want to get this bear and be on my way."

"Well, good luck, Adams," Hanson said. "I can't say that I envy you your task."

"Nor I yours," Clint replied.

Chapter Eighteen

Clint got together with Hank Pride later in the saloon to make plans.

"I'll get the supplies we need from the general store," Hank said, "and I'll supply the pack animal."

"Make sure he's steady," Clint said. "I don't want him spooking and running off with our supplies the first time he gets a whiff of that bear's scent."

"He'll be a good one, don't you worry," Hank promised.

"Good. Now there's another matter."

"What's that?" Hank asked.

"Can you shoot?"

"I can handle a rifle pretty good," Hank said. "I don't know about a handgun. Compared to you—"

"Let's not compare," Clint said. "As long as you can handle a rifle, you should be able to pull your weight."

"I've got a Henry—"

"I'll supply you with a rifle," Clint said, "but it will probably be up to me and my Parker-Hale to bring Ol' Three-Paw down for good. At the most I might need you to distract him."

"I'll do that," Hank said.

"Think you'd like a chance to wrestle him first?" Clint asked the big man.

"No, thanks," Hank said.

"Just though I'd offer."

Hank went to the bar for two more beers, came back and set Clint's down in front of him.

"Find out anything about that lady?" Hank asked.

"Which lady?"

"The one who owns that big bay mare."

"Oh, that lady," Clint said. Truth be told, he'd been thinking about her ever since he first saw her. "No, nothing. Why?"

"I heard some things," Hank said, "that's all."

"Like what?" Clint asked, with genuine interest.

"Her name is Lacy Blake," Hank said, "and the way I hear it, she's a bounty hunter."

"A bounty hunter?" Clint asked, showing his surprise. "Lacy Blake?"

"That's right."

Clint searched his memory, but the name simply did not ring any bells.

"I've never heard of her," he said.

"Well, somebody sure has," Hank said. "Fella who told me about her said he saw her in action once and she scared the hell out of him that day. She gunned a man down and didn't even blink twice."

"What was she supposed to do, cry?" Clint asked. "Who was this fella you heard from."

"Just a guy passing through," Hank assured him. "He was picking up his horse to leave town, and was talking to another man about her. I just kind of listened in."

"What else did you hear?"

"Just that she usually rides with a fella named Jake
Benteen."

"Benteen," Clint repeated. "That name I do
know."

"Who is he?"

"He's also a bounty hunter, but he's got quite a
reputation," Clint said. Suddenly he was interested in
Lacy Blake for totally different reasons.

If she normally hunted men for money, there was no
reason she shouldn't hunt a bear for five thousand
dollars.

"You look interested," Hank said.

"If she's going after that bear, I am," Clint said.
"She could be taking money out of our pockets."

"Money?"

"Oh, didn't I tell you?" Clint asked. "I arranged
with Lockman to pay you for going with me."

"Pay me?" Hank asked. "How much?"

"I don't know," Clint said. "What do you think is
fair?"

"I don't know—"

"How about five hundred?"

"Dollars?" Hank asked, widening his eyes.

"Of course dollars."

"Five hundred dollars," Hank repeated.

"Is it too much?" Clint asked.

"Huh?" Hank said, looking up at Clint. "No, no, it
ain't too much. I ain't complaining."

"Good. Why don't you start rounding up those
supplies, Hank."

"Okay," Hank agreed. He finished his beer, stood
up and asked, "When are we leaving?"

"I haven't decided yet. I still have to talk to

Lockman about something. Let's just say you should be ready to leave at a moment's notice, okay?''

"You're the boss," Hank said.

Clint finished his beer, then stood up with intentions of going to see Lockman. He wanted to know if Lacy Blake was here on her own, or if she'd been sent for by Lockman. People like her—and especially Jake Benteen—didn't usually work for hire, but Lockman seemed to have enough money to hire anyone he liked, including the Gunsmith. What was to stop him from hedging his bet by hiring Clint *and* Lacy Blake?

And Jake Benteen.

Chapter Nineteen

"I'm sorry, Clint," Calvin Lockman said, "but I don't know anyone named Blake, or Benteen."

They were in Lockman's study, and Clint had just put the question to him about Lacy Blake and Jake Benteen.

"She's probably just here in reply to the reward," Lockman said.

"I suppose it's possible," Clint admitted.

"Of course it is," Lockman said. "Now come on, have a drink."

Clint relented, only because what Lockman was offering was some of that excellent brandy.

When he had a glass in his hand Lockman asked, "When will you be going out?"

"Either tomorrow morning, or the next morning," Clint said. "It depends on how soon I can get ready."

"Have you chosen your assistant yet?"

"Yes," Clint said, "and you're paying him five hundred dollars."

"Five hundred?" Lockman asked. "You couldn't make a better deal than that?"

"You're paying me ten thousand," Clint said. "Seems to me you'd be willing to part with another five hundred if it would rid you of that grizzly."

"I suppose you're right," Lockman said. "Who is going with you?"

"Hank Pride."

"Pride," Lockman repeated. "I don't believe I know who he is."

"He runs the livery in town."

"Oh, the big fella!" Lockman said. "The one they're always paying to lift things."

"That's him."

"Well, he's certainly a powerful man," Lockman said, "but how will that help you against Ol' Three-Paw?"

"He can handle a rifle," Clint said, "and he asked to go."

"Asked?" Lockman repeated. "You mean he wants to go? And you're having me pay him—"

"He offered to help me, and I'd like to see him compensated," Clint said coldly.

"Of course, of course," Lockman said. He did not want to offend the Gunsmith, because he saw the man as his best chance to be rid of Ol' Three-Paw. "You did the right thing, of course."

"Of course," Clint said. He finished the brandy in his glass and set it down on the bar. "I've got to go."

"Certainly," Lockman said. "Tell me, when you kill the bear, what proof do you intend to bring me."

"Proof?"

"Of course," Lockman said. "You can't expect me to hand you that much money without some proof. Just as it says in the reward notice, I'll pay anyone who can kill the grizzly and bring me proof that he's dead."

"Mr. Lockman," Clint said, facing the man again, "I'm afraid that the only proof I have any intention of presenting to you is my word. Now, if that's not good enough, let me know now—''

"No, no,'' Lockman hastened to calm the Gunsmith down. "Of course your word will be proof enough. I didn't mean to imply—''

"I have to get going, Mr. Lockman,'' Clint said. "The next time I see you, Ol' Three-Paw should be dead.''

"I sincerely hope so, Mr. Adams.''

Clint walked to the door and, before opening it and going through it, turned back to Lockman and said, "Just be sure you have my money ready.''

After the Gunsmith had left, Lockman sent for one of his hands and instructed the man to go to town and tell Sheriff Hanson that he wanted to see him urgently.

When Hanson came storming into the house a little over two hours later he demanded, "How many times do you think I can ride back and forth between here and town—''

"As many times as I want you to,'' Lockman said, sharply, cutting the man off. "Remember that, Hanson. It will do you a lot of good to remember that.''

Hanson shut up and faced Lockman across the man's desk.

"Sit down,'' Lockman said, and Hanson obeyed. "There's a woman in town named Lacy Blake. What do you know about her?''

"Not much,'' Hanson said. "I understand she's a bounty hunter, works with a man named Jake Benteen. He's the one with the big reputation.''

"Is he in town with her?''

"No.''

"Well," Lockman said, "we'll have to make do with her."

"What do you mean?"

"Hanson," Lockman said, leaning forward, "I didn't get to where I am today by putting all my eggs in one basket."

"So?"

"I want you to talk to Lacy Blake for me, see if she'd be interested in hunting that grizzly down for me."

"You've got Adams for that."

"And I want Blake too. Talk to her."

"Suppose she's already here after the reward?"

"Offer her seventy-five hundred," Lockman said. "That's twenty-five hundred above the reward. That should do it."

Hanson shook his head, thinking to himself that if he had as much money as Lockman he'd be a lot more careful about how he spent it.

"I don't need your approval on this, Hanson," Lockman said sharply. "Just do what you're told."

"I'm surprised you don't just offer them money to work together," Hanson said. "Between the two of them they ought to be able to kill that thing."

Lockman frowned and said, "You might have something there, Hanson."

"I was kidding."

"I'm not," Lockman said. "If she accepts, maybe I'll make them that offer."

"Adams would never stand for it."

"For ten thousand dollars he will," Lockman said.

"You don't know him—"

"And you do?"

"I know his kind."

"And I know yours," Lockman said. "Now run

along and do what you're told, there's a good sheriff.''

Hanson hesitated, then stood up and headed for the door.

"And make sure I know as soon as you've spoken to her,'' Lockman said. Hanson turned, as if to complain about having to ride out there again, but Lockman said, "All right, send me a message if you have to, but make sure I'm told.''

Hanson put his hand on the doorknob, said, "Yes sir,'' with his back turned, and then left. His face was burning, and he swore that one day Lockman wouldn't have enough money to treat him this way and get away with it.

Later that evening Clint came down to the hotel dining room for dinner and stopped just short of entering because he spotted Lacy Blake sitting at a table with Sheriff Joe Hanson. The lady bounty hunter was the only one with a plate in front of her, so Clint doubted very much that they were dining together. He stepped out of the doorway so he wouldn't be seen but watched them for a few minutes longer. It seemed that Hanson was doing all of the talking—like a man trying to sell something.

Clint backed off all the way now and left the hotel. There were other places to eat in town, and he didn't want Hanson to know that he had seen them together just yet.

He had to find out if Hanson was trying to sell her what he thought he was trying to sell her, and then he would have to find out if she was buying.

Chapter Twenty

Clint left the hotel and walked down a few blocks to a small café to have dinner. After that he went over to the saloon to meet Hank Pride, who was waiting for him at a back table. Clint picked up two beers from the bar and went over to join him.

"Did you get the supplies?"

"Yeah," Hank said. "I've got everything over at the livery. Here's the bill," he said, handing Clint the written tally. Clint looked at it, then stuffed it in his pocket.

"I'll have Lockman take care of it," he said.

"You should have told me that before," Hank said. "I would have bought more."

"You bought plenty, Hank. With a little luck, we won't be needing any more."

Hank started to answer, but stopped when he saw that he didn't have the Gunsmith's attention. Clint was looking past him, and when Hank turned around he saw why.

Lacy Blake had walked in.

She became the center of attraction, the object of the eye of every man in the place. She walked slowly, confidently to the bar and ordered a beer. The bartender couldn't take his eyes off of her the whole time he was serving her.

When Lacy Blake had her beer she leaned on the bar and proceeded to drink it slowly. She drank like a person who has something on her mind.

Clint was about to approach her when three other men beat him to it. He sat back down.

"What's the matter?" Hank asked.

"Watch."

Hank turned around so that he could watch what happened at the bar.

The three men approached Lacy Blake, one on her left and one on her right. One of them ordered a bottle of whiskey and four glasses, and when they were set up at the bar he poured four glasses, and put one in front of Lacy Blake.

She shook her head and sipped her beer, and the same man spoke to her shortly. She responded shortly and sipped her beer again. The man became agitated and said something to his friends, who laughed. At that point the voices became loud enough for everyone in the saloon to hear.

"I guess she thinks she's too good to drink with us," the first man said.

"I guess we should show her she's wrong," the lone man on her left said. He very deliberately put one hand on her behind; he never saw the bottle coming until it crashed over his head. He went down, and she stepped back over him and drew her gun before either of the other two men knew what was happening.

"Your friend put his hand on me," she said, "and he's lucky to be alive.. Either of you want to try for unlucky?"

"Take it easy," the first man cautioned her, and the other man simply nodded. "Take it easy, lady. We was just trying to be friendly."

"Well, pick up your friend and go try it somewhere else, on someone else—and in another town!"

The two men eyed her suspiciously, as if they expected her to shoot, and when she didn't they bent down, picked up their friend and dragged him out.

Lacy Blake holstered her gun, leaned on the bar and continued to drink as if nothing happened.

"Very impressive lady," Clint said.

"I'll say," Hank agreed.

Clint got up again and Hank said, "Where you going?"

"To talk to her," Clint said.

"Don't order her no whiskey," Hank advised him. "I don't think she likes it."

"I'll remember."

Clint walked to the bar, left enough space between him and the woman for another person to fit, and ordered a beer. She never once looked over at him, but he had a feeling she knew he was there.

"That was very impressive," he said.

She didn't answer.

"I'm sure Jake Benteen would have been very proud."

This time she threw him a brief look, then returned her attention to the beer. "You know Benteen?" she asked.

"We've met once or twice. I don't know if I know him, but then I'll bet you don't either."

She looked over at him again, longer this time, and then said, "Yeah, maybe you do know him, a little. What's your name?"

"Clint Adams."

A muscle twitched beneath the smooth skin on her

cheek and he knew she recognized the name.

After a long pause she said, "Jake's mentioned you once or twice."

"I'm flattered. I wonder if we could talk."

"About what?"

"Oh, I don't know," he said. "Politics, the weather . . . grizzly bears."

She paused again, then said, "Where?"

"My friend has a table over there," he answered, jerking his head towards Hank. "We can chase him away and have a nice talk."

"Sure," she said. "Why not?"

She picked up her beer and preceded him to the table, where Hank Pride sat with wide eyes.

"Hank, this is Lacy Blake," Clint said. "This is my partner, Hank Pride."

"Big, isn't he?" she asked.

"Nice to meet you," Hank said, and he really meant it.

She looked at him again and then said, "You handle the livery, don't you?"

"That's right."

"You taking good care of my horse?"

"Real good."

"Hank," Clint said, "why don't you go over to the livery and check on her horse—and mine too while you're at it?"

"Duke's fine, Clint. I was just—"

"Hank."

"What?"

"Check on the pack animal too."

It took Hank a few more seconds, but he finally got the message that Clint wanted him to leave.

"Oh, oh, sure," the big man said, standing up. "I'll go and check on the animals. It was nice to meet you, ma'am."

"Likewise," Lacy told him.

"See you later, Clint."

"Yeah."

Hank left and Clint said, "Sit down, please. Can I get you another beer?"

"This one's fine," she said, sitting in the chair just vacated by Hank. "What did you want to talk about, specifically?"

"Ol' Three-Paw," he said. "I assume you read about the reward being offered?"

"That's why I came here," she admitted.

"And now Lockman wants to hire you personally."

"How did you know that?"

"I stopped in the hotel dining room and saw Hanson talking to you. I decided not to eat there."

"I don't blame you," she said. "He didn't do much for my appetite, either."

"How about your wallet?" Clint asked. "I'll bet he offered to do something for that."

"What's it to you?"

"Maybe I just don't like the idea of working against Jake Benteen's partner," he said. "How is Jake, anyway?"

"Jake's fine. He's resting up."

"He's not in on this with you?"

"Jake don't have any desire to bag a bear."

"And you do?"

"Five thousand buys a lot of extra bullets," she said.

"Only five?" Clint asked. "Don't tell me Lockman

didn't offer you more than that to go after Ol' Three-Paw for him.''

"What if he did?''

"I just like to know who's out there when the shooting starts,'' Clint said. "I've got some advice for you too.''

"What?''

"If you're going after that bear, you'll need something a little bigger than that Henry you were carrying earlier today.''

"That gun has always done the job for me in the past.''

"On men, yes,'' Clint said, "but not on a grizzly that weighs more than ten times what a man does. You may be out of your element here, Miss Blake.''

"Just Lacy.''

"Lacy, think about this very carefully before you decide to go ahead with it.''

"You want the money for yourself, is that it?''

"If Jake Benteen ever mentioned me, then you know better than that,'' Clint said. "I've got my own reasons for going after that bear, and they've got nothing to do with Calvin Lockman or his reward.''

She examined the beer at the bottom of her mug and then said, "All right, I'll think about it.''

"Good,'' Clint said. He stood up, which was a hard thing to do, because all he wanted right then was to remain seated there, staring at Lacy Blake's face. "If you see Jake pretty soon, tell him I was asking about him.''

"I will,'' she promised.

Clint nodded, then walked to the bar and dropped some money on it.

"If she wants another beer, take it out of that," he instructed the bartender.

When he left he spotted Sheriff Hanson across the street, probably making his rounds. He crossed over and joined him.

"I just had a nice chat with Lacy Blake," he said.

"Is that so?"

"Yeah," Clint said. "Tell Lockman for me he can hire anybody he wants, but I'm going to get that bear."

"Afraid somebody will beat you out of your money, Adams?" Hanson asked.

Thinking about Dorian Ward, a woman who thought that Ol' Three-Paw was her own personal devil, he said, "I've got my own reasons for going after that bear, Hanson, and your boss's money has nothing to do with it—but tell him to have that ten thousand right at hand, because I'm going to drop that grizzly right into his lap."

"You really think you can do it, don't you?" Hanson asked, checking a store door to be sure it was locked tight.

"Oh, I'll do it, all right, Hanson," Clint said.

Hanson stopped and faced Clint, looking into the Gunsmith's eyes. "Yeah, I'll bet you will, Adams."

"Tell Lockman I said he's wasting his money."

"It's his to waste," Hanson said. "It's his business."

"Suit yourself," Clint said. "Tell him or don't, but tell him I'll deliver. I'll be leaving in the morning."

"I'll tell him," Hanson said. Clint started across the street to the hotel, and he was halfway there when Hanson finally called out behind him, "Good luck."

● ● ●

Hank Pride slept in a small room in the back of the livery, and at about half an hour before daybreak the next morning, he was awakened by Clint Adams.

"Huh, wha—" Hank stammered, coming awake with a man's hand on his big shoulder.

"Whoa, slow down, big man," Clint said, backing away. "It's just me."

"Who?" Hank said, squinting up at Clint. "Is that you, Clint?"

"Yes, it's me," Clint said. "Jesus, but you wake up hard."

"What's going on?"

"It's time to pack up and leave."

"What time is it?"

"Sun won't come up for another half hour," Clint said. "It's time for us to go hunting."

"Nice of you to let me know in advance," Hank said, sitting up and rubbing his eyes.

"You don't have to come if you don't want to—" Clint started to say.

"I didn't say that," Hank said, cutting him off. Standing up the big man was an impressive sight. Shirtless, the muscles stood out on his arms, shoulders and chest. "Just let me wash some of this sleep out of my eyes and I'll be ready."

"I'll saddle the horses," Clint said. "Which one are you taking?"

"Saddle me the big sorrel. I'll be right there."

By the time Clint had Duke and the sorrel saddled, Hank came out dressed and ready to go. Clint gave him his own rifle, and he slid the Parker-Hale into the scabbard on Duke's saddle.

They mounted up, and the Three-Paw hunt was on.

Chapter Twenty-One

Clint and Hank spent a lot of time over the next week or so getting to know each other better, but they never even got a whiff of Ol' Three-Paw.

"How can a grizzly that size stay out of sight for a week?" Clint asked at one point.

"Maybe we ought to just settle down in one place and see if he comes to us," Hank suggested.

"You may be right, partner," Clint said. "Or maybe we ought to watch one or two of the herds nearby, and wait for him to make a move on it. He's got to get hungry sometime. I mean, a grizzly doesn't store food, does he? He's got to go after some sooner or later, right?"

"Don't ask me," Hank said. "I don't know nothing about grizzly bears, except to stay away from them."

"Then what are you doing out here?"

"Don't ask me that either."

They camped one night on the rise where Clint had first seen Ol' Three-Paw.

"What makes you think he'll come back here?" Hank asked over coffee.

"Just another way to go, Hank," Clint said. "We haven't had any luck trying to track him. I'm no tracker and neither are you, so maybe we can just get in his way.''

''Somehow I don't like the sound of that,'' Hank said.

''If we could only find that half-breed,'' Clint went on, as if he hadn't heard Hank's remark. ''What's his name?—Dusty. I'm sure he'd be able to track him for us.''

''I know Dusty,'' Hank said. ''Why ain't you mentioned him before?''

''I don't know,'' Clint said. ''The bartender mentioned him. I haven't given him that much thought until just now. What do you know about him?''

''Dusty Running Fox,'' Hank said. ''His father was white, his mother was full-blooded Comanche.''

''Comanche?'' Clint asked. ''What's he doing this far from Texas, then?''

''This is where his mother died ten years ago,'' Hank explained. ''He just stayed.''

''What about his father?''

''I don't know who he is, or if he's even still alive,'' Hank said. ''In fact, I don't even think Dusty knows.''

''How well do you know him?''

''Not well enough to find him if he don't want to be found,'' Hank answered, dumping the remains of his coffee into the fire.

''Well,'' Clint said, doing the same, ''maybe if we keep riding around in circles out here we'll run into one or the other.''

''Well, if Dusty's drunk,'' Hank said, ''running into one might be just as bad as running into the other.''

''That's great,'' Clint said. ''I thought Indians didn't drink.''

''They're not supposed to drink,'' Hank said.

"There's a difference, and the fact that he's only half Indian don't make no never mind. He gets a few drinks under his belt, he turns meaner than—than—"

"A grizzly?" Clint asked.

Hank gave Clint a steady look and then asked, "Who's got first watch?"

"It's your turn."

"I thought it was your turn," Hank said, suspiciously.

"Well," Clint said, "I was just testing you to see if you've been keeping track."

Early the next morning they were riding near the Lockman spread when they spotted a group of men standing on foot, holding the reins of their skittish horses.

"Something's up," Clint said. "Come on."

They rode onto the scene and without dismounting could see the mutilated corpse of a cow inside the circle of men.

"Hello," Clint called, and one of the men looked up. "My name's Clint Adams, this here's Hank Pride."

"I know Hank," the man said.

"What happened here, Harley?" Hank asked.

"What's it look like?" the man replied. "Ol' Three-Paw paid us a visit last night."

"Where's your herd?" Clint asked.

"About a mile that way," Harley answered, pointing north. "That grizzly snatched this cow up and carried her way the hell over here before he had his dinner."

"Jesus," Hank said.

"How long ago was the kill?" Clint asked. "Can anybody tell?"

Another man looked up and said, "I seen enough grizzly kills to guess. Couldn't've been more than an hour."

"An hour?" Hank said. He looked at Clint and said, "That's the closest we been to that son of a buck all week."

"I know it," Clint said. He looked at the group of men and asked, "Wasn't anybody on watch?"

There were five men gathered around that dead cow, and every one of them sent a look his way that was meant to kill.

"That grizzly don't care who was on watch," the man called Harley said.

"Come on, Clint," Hank said. "We better get on his trail."

"Right," Clint said. He looked at Harley and said, "Tell your boss that's the last cow he's going to lose to that bear."

"Sure," Harley said. "I'll tell him."

"Let's go," he said to Hank.

They had ridden out of sight of the five men when Hank pulled up and said, "Which way are we going?"

"South," Clint said. "That grizzly's had his breakfast and he sure as hell isn't headed back north."

"So why south?" Hank asked.

"Why not?" Clint replied.

"I've tracked men," Clint said later. "They leave behind cold campfires, cigarette butts, piss puddles, but I've never tracked a bear before."

"Well, we've seen some tracks," Hank said.

"Yeah, and we follow them, and then they disappear," Clint said. "It's as if someone was following that grizzly and wiping out his trail."

"You don't think Ol' Three-Paw can be that smart,

do you?'' Hank asked with an awed look on his face.

"He's just an animal, Hank," Clint said.

"Maybe he's watching us right now," Hank said.

"Don't be making him out to be something he's not," Clint warned. "You'll start giving yourself the jitters."

"Shoot, I've had them since you woke me up that first morning," Hank said.

When he came, he came fast and without warning.

It was getting on towards dark and they were riding up a hill, looking for a place to camp. Hank was riding in the lead, and as he reached the top of the hill, there was Ol' Three-Paw, rearing up on his hind legs. It was as if he had come up out of nowhere, and suddenly the air was filled with his angry cry. He swung one massive paw in front of him, raking the neck of Hank's sorrel, and suddenly Hank and the horse were covered with bright red blood. As the sorrel went down, the grizzly swung his other paw and took Hank right off its back. The pack horse panicked, jerked free, and fled.

It was all amazingly fast for Clint. One moment that grizzly appeared, and the next Hank was flying off the sorrel's back and landing with a sickening thud. As he went to draw the Parker-Hale the dead sorrel started rolling down the hill towards him, and it was only Duke's quickness that kept them upright. As the big black sidestepped the dead animal, the Parker-Hale came up in Clint's hand, cocked.

The bear was standing up at the top of the hill with the waning light behind him, making him look twice as large as he really was. Even Duke's usually steady nerves were jangled by that sight, and he started backing down the hill, shaking his massive head.

"Whoa, Duke," Clint said. "Steady up, boy. Give me a shot."

Hearing Clint's voice, Duke stopped backing up, but couldn't quite keep still as that grizzly suddenly started down the hill at them.

The Parker-Hale fired just two shots, and Clint didn't want to waste them. Shifting the big gun to his left hand, he drew his .45 with his right.

All of a sudden he was looking at the back of Ol' Three-Paw as the grizzly charged up the hill with incredible speed. Clint barely had a chance to get off two shots with the .45 when the bear had topped the rise and was out of sight.

"Come on, boy," Clint exhorted Duke, "we got to go after him."

Duke was more than reluctant to go back up that hill while the grizzly smell was still fresh, but under Clint's urging he grudgingly made his way to the top.

The remaining light was gone now and the other side of the hill was swathed in total darkness.

"Shit," Clint said, trying to see through the darkness. It'd be suicide to go down into that gully in the dark, after a grizzly that knew when to turn and fight, and when to turn tail and run.

Ol' Three-Paw's cry came up out of the darkness, defiant and proud, and from behind him Clint heard Hank's pitiable moan. Shoving the Parker-Hale back into its boot he looked down into the darkness again, said, "Same to you," and turned Duke around to see how badly Hank was hurt.

Chapter Twenty-Two

Clint wrapped Hank up in a blanket and made a fire right there on the side of that hill. Hank's sorrel had nearly had its head torn off, and Hank's chest had been torn open by the grizzly's claws. It would have been foolhardy to try and get Hank back to town in the dark, especially with that grizzly still prowling around. Every so often Clint could still hear him out there somewhere, so he sat by the fire with the Parker-Hale across his lap.

"Clint," Hank's voice called weakly.

"Yeah, Hank," Clint said. "I'm here."

"Where?"

"Right here, partner," he said, moving over to where Hank could see him.

"My chest hurts," Hank complained.

"I know it does, Hank."

"I'm bleeding."

"I bandaged you up as best I could, Hank," Clint said. "You'll be all right until morning, and then we'll get you back to town and have a doctor look after you."

"I'm gonna die."

"No, you're not going to die," Clint said. "The day

a big galoot like you can't stand up to a swipe from one little old grizzly. . . ."

Hank's eyes closed then, and Clint leaned forward and breathed a sigh of relief when he was able to detect the big man's breathing.

"You aren't going to die, Hank," Clint said, sitting back and laying the Parker-Hale across his lap.

Ol' Three-Paw chose that moment to cry out once again from the darkness, and Clint lifted his head up, trying to locate the direction from which it came, and said, "But you are."

At daybreak Clint lifted Hank as gently as he could onto Duke's back, preparing for the long walk back to town.

Once Hank was astride Duke he looked down at Clint and asked, "Where the hell is your shirt? Are you looking to freeze to death?"

"It's not that cold," Clint said. "Besides, my shirt is in strips, tightly wrapped around your chest."

"Oh," Hank said, "I guess that's what's keeping me from bleeding to death, huh?"

"You're going to be fine, Hank," Clint assured him. "Me and Duke will get you back to town."

"If we don't run into Ol' Three-Paw between here and there," Hank pointed out.

"Well," Clint said, reaching up, "I'll have this ready." He pulled out the Parker-Hale. "I didn't have a chance to use it last night, but that won't happen again."

"Maybe you should go ahead without me and bring back help," Hank said.

"We've already gone through that, Hank," Clint

said. "That would take twice as long, and we've got to get you to a doctor as soon as possible."

"I guess you're right," Hank said. "Maybe we'd better get a move on," he added, looking around nervously.

"Are you ready?"

"As ready as I'll ever be."

Clint picked up Duke's reins, and they started the long walk back to Bear Pass.

Chapter Twenty-Three

"You got him here just in time," the doctor told Clint, wiping his hands on a towel.

"He's going to make it?"

"Oh, yes," the doctor said. "You got him here before infection could set in, and you kept him from bleeding profusely. You saved his life."

"Sure," Clint said, "and if I had been a little quicker out there, this never would have happened."

"You can't blame yourself," the man said. He was in his late sixties, and had been the doctor in Bear Pass for more than half his life. "This bear appears to be more than just a normal grizzly."

"That's what everybody thinks," Clint said, "but I intend to prove you all wrong. I'll take care of his bill, doctor."

"We can talk about that another time. He can stay here for a while, and then you'll have to find some place for him to rest."

"He can't go back to the livery," Clint said. "I'll put him in my room back at the hotel. I won't be using it for a while."

"You're going back out there after the bear?" the doctor asked.

"As soon as I get stocked up," Clint said. "I'll be here in town for a day or so. Let me know when I can take him to the hotel."

"Tomorrow morning will be soon enough," the doctor said. "You'd better get some rest yourself. You look pretty worn out."

"I intend to, Doc," Clint said. "I'm going to be very alert when I go back out there after Ol' Three-Paw."

Clint left the doctor's office and, as much as he wanted and needed a bath, he headed straight for the saloon. The one thing he had made sure they didn't have with them was any kind of liquor, and right then he needed a drink. He felt bad about Hank getting hurt, and felt he could have prevented it if he had reacted faster to the sudden appearance of the grizzly at the top of that hill.

Over a bottle of whiskey at a back table, he reran the incident and, looking at it realistically, knew he couldn't have prevented Hank from being hurt. Hank himself was in his way at the moment that Ol' Three-Paw first appeared, and then Hank's horse was rolling down the hill towards him and Duke, spoiling any chance for a shot. Finally, even steady Duke had to react to the sight of a great grizzly charging at them, which had further ruined any chance for a true shot.

Next time it would be different, though. Duke would be steadier after the initial confrontation, and Clint himself would be quicker. That bear would not surprise him again, and this time there would be no one with him to get in the way. Having someone to back you up was useful, but having no one else to worry about was also important, and that was the way the Gunsmith was going to play it from now on. Just him and Ol' Three-Paw—and only one of them was going to walk away.

When Clint walked into the hotel lobby, Dorian was behind the counter, and when she saw him she froze.

"Hello, Dorian," he said, throwing his saddlebags up on the counter. He leaned the Parker-Hale against the front and asked, "Do I still have a room?"

"Of course," she said. "Of course you do."

"Thanks," he said. "I'm beat, and I need a bath."

"You know where it is," she said, looking down at the work she had been doing when he walked in.

He waited to see if she would look up at him again, and when she didn't, he picked up the rifle and his saddlebags and said, "Yeah, I know where it is."

He turned to walk away, then turned back. "Dorian."

"Yes?"

"I'll be going out again tomorrow, but I want to leave someone in my room until I come back."

"Who?"

"Hank Pride, the livery man," he answered.

"What happened?"

"He got hurt, and he'll need someplace to rest up. Don't worry, I'll continue to pay for the room." When she didn't answer he added, "I'll pay for a week in advance."

The suggestion seemed to annoy her. "There's no need for that. He can stay in your room as long as he needs to."

"Thank you," Clint said, and with that he turned and headed for the stairs.

"Clint," she called.

"Yes?" he said from the flight of steps.

"Did you see it?"

"Yes, I did," he said.

"Was it . . ."

When she didn't continue he said, "I don't know if it was or wasn't the same bear, Dorian, but I'm going back out there to find out."

"Alone?"

"Alone."

"You're a fool," she said, and directed her attention back to her work.

"Yeah, you're probably right," he said, only half aloud, and continued up to his room.

Chapter Twenty-Four

Clint half expected Dorian to interrupt his bath, but when she didn't he wasn't surprised. When he passed the front desk on his way back to his room, she had been replaced by the nattily dressed little man. Oddly enough, he did not expect her to be waiting for him in his room, and this time he *was* surprised.

"I want us to be together once more," she said from his bed, "before you go back out there."

"Yes," he said.

He dropped his towel to the floor, stepped out of his pants, and went to her on the bed.

She threw the sheet down so that when he laid down with her their flesh touched. Hers was burning, and she clasped herself to him as if she wanted to set him on fire.

"Fuck me, Clint, please," she said. "Do it hard, make it last!"

She was already moist and ready, and when he slammed himself into her, her sex seemed to grab his cock and hold on. When he started to pump, she wrapped her powerful, sleek legs around his waist and matched his tempo.

"Oh, God, yes!" she cried out. "Do it, you bastard, make it last, make it so I'll even feel it after that damned grizzly kills you!"

She started crying then, part from the sheer joy of their coupling, and part from grief. Whether the grief was for her dead husband, or for him, Clint didn't know, but he continued to take her in long, powerful strokes, doing what he could to make her forget the grief and remember the joy, even though he knew he'd be back, and she didn't. . . .

At breakfast he was surprised to find himself interrupted by Calvin Lockman.

"Adams," Lockman said, planting himself in front of the table.

"Mr. Lockman," Clint said. "Have a seat and join me."

"What are you doing back in town?" Lockman demanded. "Did you kill that bear?"

"No," Clint said. "I had to return with my friend. He was injured."

"By the bear?"

"Yes."

"You didn't kill it?"

"I answered that question already."

"Adams—" Lockman started, but he stopped himself, looked around to see how much attention he was getting, then sat down opposite Clint. "Adams, you weren't supposed to come back until you killed that damned grizzly. My men said they saw you on my land, where a cow was found mutilated, and that you took up the trail of Ol' Three-Paw. I assume you found him?"

Clint sipped his coffee, then said, "It was more like he found us. We scuffled, my friend was hurt, and I had to bring him back to town. I'll be leaving again as soon as I stock up on supplies."

"When will that be?"

"After breakfast, in about an hour or so," Clint said. "I'll go back out, and this time I won't come back until Ol' Three-Paw is dead."

"I hope you mean it," Lockman said, standing up. "I don't want to have to withdraw my offer to you and make you chase the reward like everyone else."

"I have my own reasons for going after that grizzly, Lockman," Clint said. "Your money is incidental."

"Money?" Lockman said. "Incidental?" The idea seemed totally unbelievable to him.

"Just go back to your ranch and stop worrying, Lockman," Clint said.

"I'll be waiting to hear from you, Adams," Lockman said. "I hope it's soon."

"It'll be however long it takes," Clint said.

Lockman hesitated, as if he wanted to say more, but then turned and left the dining room. Clint tried to finish his breakfast but his appetite was gone. He paid for his meal, and then left the hotel and walked to the general store to stock up on supplies. After that, he went to the livery and, dealing with the man Hank had left in charge, arranged for another pack horse. If he got lucky, he'd find the first one wandering around somewhere, still alive.

As Clint was about to leave the temporary livery-man, George Doherty, said, "There might be something you should know, Mr. Adams, before you go back out there."

"What's that?"

"Well, that lady, the one with the red hair?"

"Lacy Blake?"

"Yeah, that's the one."

"What about her?"

"Well, she came in here and couple of days after you and Hank left and rented a horse to use as a pack animal."

"Did she?" Clint asked. "I don't suppose she was stocking up for a long trip, like to New Mexico?"

"Not a chance," George said. "She's out there, where you and Hank were. I'm surprised you didn't run into her."

"So am I," Clint replied. "In fact, I'm surprised we didn't run into anyone going after that reward."

"There ain't nobody out there but you and the Blake lady," George said. "A few people came to town, but when they heard about Ol' Three-Paw, even five thousand dollars wasn't enough to get them out there."

"Interesting," Clint said. "Lockman's reward is not receiving the attention he anticipated."

"And he ain't very pleased about it, I can tell you that."

The idea of Calvin Lockman being displeased and disappointed somehow appealed to Clint, but the idea of Lacy Blake being out there alone, hunting Ol' Three-Paw, didn't.

"I assume she went out there alone," he said.

"As far as I know," George said. "Unless she met somebody outside of town."

Could that be? Clint thought. *Did she leave town and meet Jake Benteen? Are both of them out there, hunting for Ol' Three-Paw?* He didn't think so. There was no reason that he could see for Lacy Blake to lie about Jake Benteen's whereabouts. No, that lady wouldn't blink at the prospect of facing a grizzly bear on her own.

"Thanks for the information, George."

"What about big Hank? Is he going to be all right?"

"He'll be fine," Clint said. "I'm going to take him from the doctor's office now to my room, and he can get plenty of rest there."

"I'll look in on him from time to time," George promised.

"I'm sure that'll help, George. Thanks. I'll be in later to load up the pack animal."

"Don't worry about that," George said. "I'll handle that for you."

"Thanks again, George."

"You just get that bear, Mr. Adams," George said. "Folks hereabouts are talking about leaving town because of Ol' Three-Paw. I'd hate to see this turn into a ghost town."

"So would I, George," Clint said, clasping a hand on the man's shoulder. "So would I."

Clint left the livery and walked back to his hotel room. He wanted to pack his saddlebags and pick up the Parker-Hale, and then go over and get Hank from the doctor's office. After that, he'd head out again, after Ol' Three-Paw, and he'd be on the lookout for Lacy Blake. The lady may not have been afraid to face a grizzly alone, but if she did, he was sure she was going to find out that she had bitten off way too large a bite to chew.

That is, if Ol' Three-Paw didn't chew her up, first.

Chapter Twenty-Five

The Gunsmith was used to riding alone and he found now that without Hank Pride along he was much more relaxed—or as relaxed as he could be with Ol' Three-Paw running around out there. Being more relaxed, he also felt more alert, which was very important. Still, as alert as he was for any sign of the big grizzly, there was a portion of his mind that was thinking about Lacy Blake.

With the reputation that she had as Jake Benteen's partner Clint had no doubt that the woman had a cool, keen mind and the ability to handle almost any situation that might come her way, but he couldn't help but wonder how she would react when she came face to face with Ol' Three-Paw.

Clint also did some studying on his own reaction upon coming face to face with the big grizzly. With the waning light, and the shadows, it would have been very hard for him to accurately figure the size of Ol' Three-Paw, but he knew that the grizzly was much larger than the seven foot Sasquatch had been, and that creature had been very hard to find and finally kill.*
The massive animal beneath him was testimony

---

*The Gunsmith #21: Sasquatch Hunt

110

enough to the obvious danger presented by the great bear. Duke, normally a cool customer himself, had backed away from the creature, and might even have run had it not been for Clint's smooth handling. The Gunsmith had never seen the big animal react that way before.

Having come that close to the grizzly, Duke would certainly be able to pick the beast's scent up early next time, and give Clint some advance warning.

By the time Clint had picked Hank up from the doctor's and gotten him settled in the hotel, it was later than he normally would have left. Now, as darkness fell, he felt as if he had been in the saddle since sunup. He found a likely place to camp, built a fire and kept Duke very near, so that the big black could warn him if the grizzly scent caught his attention.

He was on his second pot of coffee when Duke suddenly lifted his massive head and sniffed at the air.

"What is it, boy?" Clint asked, picking the Parker-Hale up from his lap. "You smell that grizzly?"

Duke continued to sniff at the air. Clint stood up, holding the big gun ready, peering into the darkness. Before long, he was able to hear whoever or whatever it was that Duke had heard and smelled long before.

"All right," Clint shouted, "who's out there?"

There was a long silence, during which Clint imagined Ol' Three-Paw suddenly charging out of the darkness at him while he raised the Parker-Hale and—

"Hold the fire!" It was a woman's voice, strong but with an edge of fatigue.

"If you don't have a bear with you, come on in," Clint called back.

The caller stepped out of the brush and moved closer

to the fire, leading her horse, and Clint recognized Lacy Blake and her big mare.

"Adams," she said, stopping a few feet out from his fire.

"Miss Blake," he greeted. "You look terrible."

"Thanks."

Actually, she did look terrible. Her clothes were filthy, as was her face, and the backs of her hands had been scraped. The fatigue showed in her face and in the slump of her shoulders, but aside from all of that, she was the loveliest thing he had seen in weeks.

"You look like you could use some coffee," he said.

"And something to eat, if you can spare it."

"There's plenty," he said. "Sit and have some."

"Thanks."

She picketed her horse next to Duke, and the big gelding turned his head away from the mare.

"What is he, antisocial?" she asked.

"He's a gelding," Clint said. "He's got no use for fillies or mares."

She sat down at the fire and he handed her a cup of coffee and a plate of beans.

"I hope you don't mind the beans," he said.

"It looks like a full-course meal to me," she said. "I ran short of supplies yesterday."

"Why didn't you go back to town for more?"

In between hungry swallows she said, "I was on that grizzly's trail and I didn't want to give it up."

"Did you catch up to him?" Clint asked.

"Once," she said. She paused for a moment and said, "He was so huge!"

"Did you fire at him?"

She looked sheepish and said, "I was so surprised at

the size of him that I didn't fire until it was too late. I might have hit him, but I can't be sure."

"When was this?"

"Yesterday."

"That's after we had our run in with him."

"You took a shot at him too?"

He nodded, and went on to explain to her just what had happened, and why he had to go back to town.

"The only good thing was that I was able to stock up on supplies again."

"I guess I'll have to go back," she said, "unless . . ."

"Unless what?"

"Look," she said, putting the plate of beans on her lap so she could use her hands while she spoke, "we're both working for Lockman, right?"

"Wrong," he said. "I've got my own reasons for going after that grizzly, not the least of which is what he did to Hank Pride."

"All right," she said, "so you want revenge, and I want money. We are after the same thing, though, in the end."

"Ol' Three-Paw," Clint said.

"Right."

"You're proposing that we throw in together?"

"Right again," she said. "With that cannon, you've got a better chance of bringing that bear down, and we both collect from Lockman."

"Wait a minute," Clint said. "My guess is that I'm throwing my supplies and my gun into the deal, but what are you contributing to this partnership?"

She sipped her coffee and then said, "I can track the animal—can you?"

"I'm not a tracker, and never have been," he said.

"Well, in my business, you learn," she said.

"Especially when you're working with Jake Benteen."

"That's right."

"Are you sure Jake's not out there somewhere?" Clint asked.

"I told you before," she said, "Jake has no desire to hunt down a bear."

"He may be missing quite a challenge."

"I think he is. Can I have some more coffee?"

"Sure."

He poured her another cup and she asked, "What about it, Clint? Can I call you Clint?"

"Sure, why not?" he said.

"You can call me Lacy," she said, "since we're going to be partners for a while. We are going to be partners, aren't we?"

He poured himself some coffee and studied her over the rim of his cup.

"Well," he said, finally, "I guess it couldn't hurt—for a while."

Chapter Twenty-Six

After the agreement was struck Clint settled back with the Parker-Hale across his lap and listened to Lacy Blake's story of her encounter with Ol' Three-Paw. . . .

Lacy did just what Clint and Hank had done—rode around for a couple of days, trying to pick up some sign of the grizzly, but where Clint and Hank had virtually ridden into Ol' Three-Paw, she had succeeded in picking up his trail, and started to track him.

"I was able to adjust to the fact that I was tracking an animal," she said, "and not a man. Jake taught me to read sign almost as well as he can. I tracked that big beast for days, lost him, and then picked up the trail again—only this time it was different."

"How?"

"He wasn't moving as fast, as confidently," she said, "and now I know why."

It was during the time that she had lost him that Clint and Hank had run into Ol' Three-Paw, and apparently Clint had hit the grizzly with at least one shot.

"Not a killing shot," she said, "but he bled, and I found signs of it. That was how I picked up the trail again."

So now Lacy Blake was tracking a wounded grizzly,

which made the beast even more dangerous.

"This is the part that . . . that scares me," she said. She hesitated a moment before admitting to him that she had felt a touch of fear.

"What?"

"He was *waiting* for me," she said. "I tracked him into a canyon a few miles from here. I thought it was a box canyon, but he went in, so I had to go in too."

She dismounted and led her horse into the canyon mouth. She was afraid that if she left the animal alone and she got wind of the grizzly's scent, she might bolt and run.

"Being left afoot scared me even more," she confided.

"It would scare me too," he admitted.

She entered the canyon with her Henry and the horse's reins in her left hand, and her right hand hovering near her holstered .45.

"Once inside, I mounted up again and we searched that canyon, Clint, from one end to the other, and that grizzly wasn't there."

"But you said it was a box."

"I thought it was," she said, "and I didn't find out different for sure until we started to leave."

In order to get out of the canyon, she had to dismount and lead her horse through the rocky, narrow mouth again. As they were coming to the outside, a large shape suddenly stepped in their path, and Clicker reared.

"She pulled her reins free, and she also knocked my rifle from my grasp," she went on. "Clint, that grizzly lured me into that canyon, knew another way out, and then waited for me at the mouth."

"That's giving an animal a lot of credit," Clint said.

"How would you explain it, then?"

"Maybe he never went into the canyon."

"I tracked him into that canyon, Clint," she insisted.

"All right."

"He was huge," she said. "Monstrous! Ten, maybe twelve feet standing straight up on his hind legs."

Clint thought back to the night he and Hank had encountered the grizzly, and he had thought the animal looked so huge because of the shadows.

"And all I had was my forty-five," she added.

"Even a well-placed shot with a forty-five—" Clint started to say.

"I didn't get a chance," she broke in. "He waited until I was within his reach before he showed himself. He reached out with one huge paw and pushed me back."

"He took a swipe at you?"

"No, he *pushed* me. Look," she said. She put down her coffee cup and opened the top two buttons of her shirt to reveal the creamy swell of her breasts. There were several puncture marks marring the perfection of her skin, but there were no claw marks.

"Punctures," she said, closing the shirt, "not scratches. He pushed me. If the animal had taken a swipe at me he would have torn me open."

"I suppose you're right," Clint said, puzzling over the bear's actions. "So why didn't he?"

"I don't know," she said, showing that she was just as puzzled as he was.

"What happened next?"

"He backed off," she said. "He disappeared from sight, and I was sure he was waiting for me to try and leave so he could take my head off."

"What did you do then?"

"I started to remember that if he had found another way out, he could find the same way in again. He could have been behind me, or in front of me . . ."

"But he couldn't be in both places at one time."

"Right," she agreed, "so I went after Clicker. Luckily, she hadn't wandered far. All she wanted to do was get out of that confined space. I gathered up her reins and had a hell of a time convincing her to follow me again, but I finally made it. I picked up my rifle, held the reins in one hand and the Henry in the other, and we walked out of that canyon."

"And?"

"And Ol' Three-Paw was nowhere to be seen. I camped a few yards from the canyon mouth, hoping to catch him when he came out again, but he never did."

"He never went back into the canyon."

"Apparently not," she said. "He left me sitting there all night, while he put a lot of distance between him and me. The next morning I decided that I needed more supplies if I was going to track him again, and here I am. . . .

"I blew it," she went on. "If I had taken a pack horse with supplies, instead of just jamming my saddlebags full, I'd have been able to continue following him. Now the trail has gone cold."

"But you can pick it up again, can't you?" he asked.

She smiled and said, "Just as soon as it gets light."

They finished off the beans and coffee, and then Clint made another pot to last them through the night as they alternated two-hour watches.

He showed her how to use the Parker-Hale and warned her that it only held two shots.

"But that doesn't mean you can miss with the first," he said.

"I'll try not to," she promised. "I'll take the first watch."

"No, I'll take it," he said. "You look beat."

"I feel beat," she said. "There's only one thing about not going back to town that makes me sorry."

"What?"

"I was intending to take a nice, long bath," she said, "and now I'll have to wait."

"Not necessarily," he said. "There's a stream not far from here. We can stop there in the morning."

"That'll take some time away from us," she warned.

"I'm sure you'll be a much better tracker when you're more comfortable," he said. Taking the Parker-Hale back from her he said, "Get some rest now, and I'll wake you in two hours."

Lacy stretched out on her blanket, with her head on her saddle, and Clint turned towards the fire and poured himself a cup of coffee.

"Lacy," he said, suddenly.

"What?"

"You were pretty close to Ol' Three-Paw, weren't you?"

"Close enough for me to feel his breath," she said.

"Did you notice if he had a streak of gray hair on his right shoulder?"

There was a moment's pause, and then Lacy said, "I didn't notice that. Why do you ask such an odd question?"

"Never mind," he said. "Go to sleep. I want you bright-eyed and alert come morning."

Chapter Twenty-Seven

When Lacy woke Clint for his second watch, she looked so terrible that he decided to let her sleep out the night. When he finally woke her she asked, ''My watch already?''

''Bath time,'' he said.

''What?'' she asked, sitting up. ''What time is it?''

''Time to get moving,'' he said. ''I've already saddled the horses.''

''You let me sleep the rest of the night?'' she asked.

''You needed it more than I did,'' he said.

She rubbed her hand over her face and said, ''I don't know what to say. Partners share everything equally.''

''Is that what Jake Benteen taught you?'' he asked.

''That's one thing, yes,'' she said. She actually seemed to be getting angry over the fact that he had let her sleep.

''Well, don't get all upset about it, Lacy,'' he said. ''My motives were purely selfish. Let's get our roles in the partnership straight. You're the tracker, and I'm the trigger. Like I said last night, I want you alert.''

When he put it that way, some of her anger abated, even though she didn't totally believe the part about his motives being purely selfish.

Getting to her feet she said, "Maybe we should forget the bath."

"I don't think so," he said. "In fact, I'm starting to smell pretty ripe myself." He mounted Duke and, looking down at Lacy said, "I just may join you."

He rode off then, leaving her standing there with her hands on her hips. Looking over at Clicker, she wondered then how the hell Clint had gotten her saddle from beneath her head without waking her.

Maybe he was right. Maybe she *had* needed the extra sleep—and she would also concede the bath, because it too might be something she needed in order to get the job done. After the bath, though, she was going to make sure that this relationship was a partnership all the way down the line—and she was going to make sure that Clint Adams knew it.

When the Gunsmith began to remove his boots Lacy Blake looked at him and said, "I thought you were kidding."

"If you're shy," he said, removing his socks, "you can take yours after I'm done."

They were standing at the edge of the stream, and as he began to unbutton his shirt, she walked up to him and, pushing his hands away, said, "I'll show you who's shy."

She continued to unbutton his shirt for him, looking him straight in the eye.

"I guess you think you're pretty smart," she said.

"Oh, I've had my days," he said, as she slid one hand inside his shirt.

"I'll bet you I can show you something you haven't seen before," she whispered, wetting her lips with a quick motion of her tongue.

"Oh, yeah?" he asked. "What's that?"

"A new way to take a bath," she said, "and wash your clothes at the same time."

She put both hands against his chest and pushed with all her might. Clint went tumbling backwards, trying to keep his balance, and came to rest sitting in the middle of the stream with his clothes on.

Lacy Blake, fully dressed herself, then jumped in after him.

Chapter Twenty-Eight

"Still smell ripe?" she asked a half hour later.

"No," Clint said, "and I'm dry already, but that doesn't mean I forgive you. You could have gotten my gun wet."

Only the fact that he had twisted his body around as he fell into the water had kept his modified .45 from getting wet, and he still intended to clean it first chance he got.

"I guess that's pretty serious, in your book, huh?" she asked.

"It should be in yours too," he said, "especially the kind of business you're in, and the man you learned it from."

"You've got a lot of respect for Jake, don't you?" she asked.

"Sure I do," he said.

"He's got a lot of respect for you too."

"That's fine."

"I'm sorry I pushed you in the water," she said.

"That's okay," he said. "I told you I needed a bath, anyway."

"I just didn't want you to think you could, uh—"

"Lacy, I understand," he said.

"It's just the way I work, Clint," she said. "We're

partners, now, and I have to keep things on the business level.''

"Sure," he said.

They rode in silence for a while, with Clint thinking about Ol' Three-Paw, when Lacy suddenly broke the silence.

"You're wondering about Jake, right?" she asked.

"What?"

"You're thinking about Jake and me, aren't you?"

"I was thinking about the bear."

"You're wondering if we have separate bedrolls, right?"

"The bear, Lacy," he said. "I was thinking about the bear, and if you'll let me, I'll go back to thinking about it."

"Fine," she said.

"Fine."

Now that she was keeping quiet, all he could think about was Lacy Blake and Jake Benteen. Could a man and woman ride together for as long as they had and keep it on a strictly nonphysical level? It was hard for Clint to imagine, because he himself had never had that kind of a relationship with a woman.

"Still thinking about the bear?" she asked, breaking into his thoughts.

"Huh? Oh, yeah, still thinking about him," he replied.

"Do you think that gun of yours will stop him?"

"It'll blow a hole through him, I'm sure of that," he said. "But if he's as big as you say, I don't know if it will stop him. I guess I'll just have to put both shots where they'll do the most good."

"Well, if I can throw a few into him at the same

time," she said, "I'm sure we'll be able to bring him down together."

"Let's just keep thinking that way," he said.

They rode on some more, and then Lacy starting talking again. "Clint, how are we going to prove to Lockman that we killed this bear so we can collect?"

"Do you talk Benteen's ear off this way when you ride with him?" he asked. She glared at him and he said, "All right. I told Lockman that all I was giving him was my word, and he went along with it."

"He's going to hand over that kind of money just on your word?" she asked.

"He said he would."

"You don't believe him?"

"Let's just say that the man didn't make his money by giving it away on somebody's say-so."

"So then why are you going through with it?"

"I told you I had my reasons."

"Yeah, but what are they?" she asked. "I'm only after this beast for the money."

"Then lop off his ears when we get him and bring them back to Lockman."

"But why are you after it?"

"It's just something I feel I have to do," he said. "This animal has hurt too many people already."

"And killed a lot of stock too, the way I heard it," Lacy said.

"That too."

"Is it because of what he did to your friend Hank?"

"Yes," Clint said, because he thought it would be the quickest way to get her to drop the subject.

He didn't want to have to explain to her that there was a woman back in Bear Pass who saw this grizzly as her own personal demon and that by killing the creature he hoped to free her.

Would Lacy Blake, the bounty hunter, understand that?

"Well," Lacy said then, "if you didn't want to talk about it, all you had to do was say so."

"Can I ask a question now?" Clint asked later.

"Ask away."

"Where are we headed?"

"Back to that canyon where I had my run-in with Ol' Three-Paw," she said.

"Will you be able to pick up the trail from there?"

"Well, I can't pick it up from here," she snapped.

"Lacy—"

"Do you always ask so many questions when you ride with someone?" she asked.

"I rarely ride with anyone," Clint said, "and I'm starting to regret that this is one of those rare occasions."

"When I track that grizzly and you get your shot at him," she said, "tell me if you still regret it."

"Sure," Clint said, "providing you are able to find him again."

"And," she added, "providing that you don't miss."

"If I do," he said, "we'll both have an opportunity to regret it."

"I heard that the Gunsmith never misses."

"You ride with Jake Benteen," he reminded her. "You of all people should know that you can't always believe everything you hear."

Lacy Blake bit her lip at the reprimand. "All right. Let me do my part and find that grizzly, and then you can do yours and we can dissolve this . . . this . . . *partnership.''*

Clint had heard a lot of obscenities over the years, but none had sounded so distasteful as when Lacy Blake said the word *partnership.*

Chapter Twenty-Nine

When they reached the canyon where Lacy had been pushed by Ol' Three-Paw, Clint inspected the entrance and then said, "I see what you meant. There wasn't really any place for you to go, was there?"

"Just front or back," she said. She peered through the narrow entrance and asked, "Do you think we should go in and check?"

"I'll check, and you look around and see if you can find some sign."

"Don't you want me to back you up?"

"You wouldn't be able to do much from right behind me, anyway," he said. "Of course, you could make sure that he doesn't come in after me," he added, as an afterthought.

"I don't think we have to worry either way," she said. "He's long gone from here."

"I'll go in and look, anyway," he said.

"Be careful."

"Right."

He hefted the Parker-Hale, and then stepped through the narrow entrance to the canyon. The ground was solid rock, and Clint was convinced that this wasn't really an entrance to the canyon, but a crack that had sometime or other appeared in the canyon wall. That meant that the main entrance had to be somewhere else. It also meant that Ol' Three-Paw had deliberately led Lacy in this way, so he could double back on her and catch her in the confined space.

That thought sent a chill up his spine, and then back down again.

Holding the Parker-Hale tightly he stepped out of the crack and into the canyon, which turned out to be pretty small, as canyons go. The presence of a grizzly would have made it seem a lot smaller, but Ol' Three-Paw was nowhere to be seen.

Clint decided to walk around and see if he could spot the other entrance. It didn't take him very long before he saw it, and it wasn't all that much larger than the one he had come through. The ground was loose dirt, though, and not solid rock, and the imprint of a giant grizzly's paws were as plain as day. If Lacy was going to have a chance of picking up Ol' Three-Paw's trail, this was the place to start.

Doubling back to his point of entry, Clint came across something else which explained what the grizzly had been using the canyon for.

When he got back to the crack he heard Lacy calling to him from the other end, and she sounded more than a bit frantic.

"Coming through," he called back.

As he came out the other end she said, "Where the hell were you? I was just about to come in after you."

"Did you find any sign of him?" he asked.

"No. It's all rocky here, there's no way to pick up any prints or sign."

"Well, get back on your horse and come with me," he said. "I've got something to show you."

They both mounted up and he led her around to the main entrance to the canyon.

"What's this?" she asked.

"This is how that bear got in and out of here," he said. "He brought you through the back entrance."

"So he *did* know exactly where he was taking me," she said.

"It seems like it," he said, dismounting. "Come on, I'll show you something else."

He knew that the canyon was empty, but he brought the Parker-Hale with him, anyway.

She followed him back into the canyon on foot and he showed her Ol' Three-Paw's reasons for using the canyon.

"What the hell is that?" she asked, making a face.

"That's his food supply," he told her.

On the ground in front of them were various parts from various different cows and horses, as well as some smaller animals—and one human arm.

"You mean he was bringing me here to add me to his supply?" she asked.

"I guess that's one way of looking at it," Clint said. "Come on, there are plenty of tracks back by the entrance. You should be able to pick up his trail."

"Sure," she said. She took one last look at Ol' Three-Paw's food supply, and then followed Clint.

"Listen," she said, "why don't we just sit here and wait for him to get hungry?"

"Look, we've already agreed that this bear is smarter than the average bear, right?"

"I guess."

"He didn't get you, so he's not going to come back here and let you take a free shot at him."

"So where's he going to go?"

"I don't know," he said. "Your part of this deal is to find him, so start looking."

Clint walked over to Duke and mounted up while Lacy walked around in circles, studying the tracks on the ground.

"They tell you anything?" he asked.

"Yeah," she answered, without looking up. "He was big, and he was hungry."

An animal that big has got to be hungry all the time, Clint told himself. He took Lacy's hint and kept quiet while she continued to study that ground.

Finally, she looked up, walked to Clicker and mounted up.

"Well?"

"Let's head north and see what it gets us," she suggested.

"That sounds like a guess," he said.

"If it is, it's an educated one," she answered. "Like you said, he's not going to come back here."

"What about Bear Pass?"

She frowned and then asked, "Is there anyone else out looking for him?"

"Not a one," he said. "The legend of Ol' Three-Paw seems to have scared away everyone but us."

"Well," she said, thinking about that, "he's still been shot at twice in a few days, and he led me into a trap. He knows somebody's after him, Clint. I don't think he'll head back towards Bear Pass."

"What do you think?"

"I think he'll lead us on until he gets us where he wants us," she said. "Then he'll kill us."

"Or try to," Clint said. "It's going to be one way or the other, Lacy, and we aren't going to find out which just standing here."

"Well," Lacy said, as if she were surprised, "we agree on something." She turned Clicker and headed north, and Clint pointed Duke in that direction and followed her.

Chapter Thirty

"While you were in town," Clint asked, "did you hear anything about a half-breed named Dusty?"

"Sure," she said. "Somebody told me he'd seen the grizzly a couple of times. I looked for him, but I couldn't find him."

"He's supposed to be holed up somewhere out here," Clint said. "Goes into town very rarely."

"So?"

"Don't you think it's odd that neither one of us has run into him out here?"

"Maybe he doesn't want to be run into."

"Maybe not," he said, "but maybe we should make a point of looking for him."

"Why?"

"No reflection on your tracking abilities, Lacy, but maybe we could persuade him to help us."

She frowned and looked over at him. "Are you trying to cut me out of this deal now, Mr. Adams? That's no way to treat a partner."

"You seem to set a lot of store in that word, Lacy," he said.

"What word?"

"Partner, partnership," he said.

"You work with a partner, your life depends on him," she said.

"Or her?"

"That's right," she answered. "Or her."

"Learned that from Jake Benteen too, I'll wager."

"That's right," she said. "When I partner up with someone, I expect him to watch my back, just as I'll watch his. I also expect him to share everything with me—everything that we go into together, that is."

"The money that you get from this hunt—will you share that with Benteen?"

"You don't see him here, do you?" she asked. "He had a chance to come along, and he decided not to."

"But you'll meet up with him later on?"

"That's right," she said. "We're partners."

"There must be something pretty special about you, Lacy," Clint said.

She looked at him sharply and said, "What do you mean by that?"

"Not what you think," he answered. "I always heard that Jake Benteen worked alone."

"He did," she said, "for years."

"And then he met you."

"That's right."

"And now you're partners."

"Right again."

"What happened in between?" he asked. "That's what I meant about you being something special. To meet a man who's ridden alone for so many years and make him take you on as a partner—"

"I didn't make Jake do anything," she said. "Nobody makes Jake do anything."

"No, I guess not," Clint said. "So, what happened in between?"

"What happened is no business of yours."

"But we're partners."

"Just for this one hunt," she said. "That doesn't entitle you to know my life story."

"No," Clint said, "I guess it doesn't."

They rode half a day, and then stopped to rest the horses.

"Have you seen any sign?" he asked.

"Here and there," she said, "but doesn't mean that it was left by Ol' Three-Paw."

"So, we could be going in the wrong direction."

"Or the right direction," she added.

"We're pretty far from Bear Pass right now."

"So?" she said. "You want to head back?"

"No, I guess we can keep going a bit longer," he said. "At one point or another, though, we're going to have to decide that we made the wrong decision."

"That's my job," she said. "I'll let you know when we reach that point."

"Fine," he said.

"Let's get going," she said. "That big black of yours can't need more rest than this."

"Duke?" Clint asked. "I thought we stopped so you could rest your horse."

"Clicker?" she said. "She doesn't need rest after an afternoon's jog like this."

"Well, neither does Duke."

"Then let's get going," she said, mounting up. "The sooner we kill that bear the sooner we can—"

"—dissolve this partnership," Clint finished for her. "I heard you the first time."

Chapter Thirty-One

The creature stared down from his vantage point on a hilltop and watched the man and the woman sit by the fire, drinking coffee and speaking to each other.

The bear was standing on all fours, with the stump of the missing fourth paw dangling above the ground. His fur was buff colored, with silvery tips. His eyes were large and brown, and were fixed on the two people. They were following him, and meant him harm. This was all the beast needed to know. Soon he would stop running and turn to face them, but not until his instincts told him that the time and place were right. He would watch them all night, and at first light he'd start out again, with them following right behind.

The man standing next to the bear was half Indian and half white. He stood with one hand on the bear's massive, humped shoulders.

"They still follow, Great One," he said. "Soon, you will turn and crush them, for they are the enemy."

The bear stood impassive, not reacting to either the man's touch, or the sound of his voice. The half-breed known as Dusty could feel his chest swell with pride whenever the Great One allowed him near, for he knew that he was the only human whose presence, whose touch, the Great One would tolerate.

He took his hand off the grizzly's shoulders now and stepped away.

"You will watch them all night," Dusty said. "You will not sleep, but I will sleep, and through me you will gain the rest you need."

Convinced that if he slept, the great grizzly would be refreshed come morning, the breed lay down on the hard ground, put his head on his arms, and went to sleep.

Ol' Three-Paw continued to watch, oblivious of the sleeping human.

Chapter Thirty-Two

"I tell you I feel like I'm being watched," Lacy said again.

"It's possible," Clint said. "Maybe that grizzly is out there somewhere, watching us."

"I suppose he's waiting for us to start after him again?" Lacy asked.

"Maybe," Clint said. "If he's capable of leading you to that canyon, then he's capable of leading us on a chase, and then trying to kill us."

After a few moments she said, "It feels different."

"What feels different?"

"Tracking a man and tracking an animal," she said. "They're different, you know?"

"In what way?"

"Well, you ought to know," she said. "You were a lawman for a lot of years."

"So?"

"So, you've tracked men before."

"It was my job," he said. "I didn't feel anything while I was chasing them. What do you feel?"

"When me and Jake are tracking somebody?"

He nodded.

"Excited," she said. "I feel . . . I don't know, I feel anticipation. I can't wait until we catch up to them and try to take them."

"You want them to resist?"

"No, of course not," she answered, a little too quickly for his money. "You think I'm looking for an excuse to kill the men I hunt?"

"You only hunt men?"

"No!"

"When's the last time you hunted a woman, then?"

"I—we never hunted a woman," she admitted, then added, "But that doesn't mean we wouldn't if the price was right."

"Okay," he said. "So tell me why it feels different to be hunting an animal."

"I don't know," she said, looking puzzled. "There's no excitement, no anticipation. I mean, I want to catch up to it and get this over with, but it doesn't go beyond that."

"You're scared, aren't you?" he asked.

She stared at him for a few moments and then finally admitted, "Yeah, I'm scared, Clint, and I don't like the feeling. There ain't a man alive who can make me feel scared, but that grizzly does."

"That's nothing to be ashamed of, honey," he said, feeling closer to her than he had since meeting her. "I'm scared too. Scared of what could happen when we catch up to that beast—or when he lets us catch up to him."

She stared at him across the fire, and he watched the flames light up her red hair, as if it were glowing.

"Maybe we can keep each other from being scared, Clint," she said. "Do you think we can do that?"

He paused a moment, considering her proposal, wondering if she meant what it sounded like she meant.

"We're partners," he reminded her. "You said—"

"I know what I said, damn it!" she snapped.

"Clint, I ain't never been this scared before."

"Okay, Lacy," he said. "Okay."

He stood up, walked around the fire, and sat down next to her, and they proceeded to do their best to make the other forget their fears, at least for one night.

Chapter Thirty-Three

When he kissed her, she thrust her tongue into his mouth, and when he started undoing the buttons of her shirt, she shivered in spite of the heat from the fire.

When he pushed her down on her back, she went willingly, and clutched him to her eagerly. With matching intensity, they removed each other's clothes, and then his lips were tasting her nipples, and kissing the fair skin of her breasts, carefully avoiding the sore wounds left by Ol' Three-Paw's claws.

"Oh, Clint," she breathed as he sucked her coppery brown nipples to incredible hardness. She reached between them and wrapped her fingers around his rigid organ and pulled it towards the damp portal between her legs.

"Now, Clint," she said. "I want it now, please."

He raised his hips a little bit, and she pointed his penis so that, with a sharp movement of his hips, he bulled his way past her soft, wet lips and plunged into her as deeply as he could.

As he drove into her with brutal strokes, all thoughts of grizzly bears and hunted men fled from her mind, and she was only aware of the intense pleasure that was burning its way through her loins.

"Oh, yes," she cried out at the top of her lungs.
"Yes, yes . . ."

As Clint felt her soft belly begin to tremble in anticipation of her orgasm, he felt his own climax building to
the point where he would not be able to contain it.
Suddenly, she began to writhe and buck beneath him,
sucking her breath in, and he knew that it was time to
let himself go. As he filled her with his white hot seed,
she screamed, and he allowed himself a fleeting moment to be thankful that they were out in the middle of
nowhere.

"God," she said after a few moments.

He kissed her, and as she moved her lips, he felt
himself starting to swell within her.

"You're still hard," she said, running her hands
over his butt, "and getting harder."

"I've been hard since the first time I saw you," he
told her.

"Liar," she said, slapping his ass, "but I like it.
Turn over."

"What—"

"Turn over, Clint," she said, licking her lips. "I
want you in my mouth."

"Lacy—" he said, showing surprise. He wouldn't
have expected that this wanton creature on her knees,
hovering above him, existed inside of Lacy Blake, the
bounty hunter. He would never have bet on it.

"Now," she said, eyes glowing. She lowered her
head until her tongue flicked out, laving the swollen tip
of his cock avidly. When she took him into her mouth,
he tensed at the exquisite pleasure of it, closing his eyes
as she began to suck on him.

"Lacy," he said, running his fingers through her
long hair, gripping her head as it bobbed up and down,

as her mouth sucked a second torrent of semen from him.

"Did you think I was a virgin," she asked later, "just because of what I said about keeping a partnership all business?"

"No, of course not," he said.

They were lying together by the fire, wrapped together in one blanket, still naked, still enjoying the feel of each other while they recaptured their breath.

"Of course not," he said again. "I just wouldn't have expected—I mean, I didn't think—"

"You didn't think there was a woman inside the bounty hunter," she said. "I know I act tough, Clint. I know a lot of people who have thought that I got into this business because I wish I was a man—"

"Jesus, I'm glad you're not," he said, tightening his arms around her.

"Oh, so am I," she said, "and I always have been. That's not why I became a bounty hunter at all."

That was his cue to ask why, but he refrained from doing so. He didn't want her to think that, just because they were lying there together, naked, she should open herself up to him totally.

She touched his chin with her finger and said, "You didn't ask."

"I know."

"Why not?"

"There's no reason you should tell me," he said.

"Not even what we just . . . had?"

"What we just shared was one thing, Lacy," he said, "and I hope we'll share it again, but realistically speaking, it doesn't mean much past tonight, past this moment. If and when you feel that there's something you want to tell me, something you want to share, I'll be ready to listen, but don't ever feel obliged to tell me anything.''

She kissed his cheek gently, like a sister, and said, ''You're pretty special yourself, you know?''

''Sure I know,'' he said.

''Did you mean what you said about wanting it to happen again?'' she asked.

''You bet I did,'' he answered. ''Why?''

''Because I feel the same way,'' she told him, moving her hands around beneath the blanket until she found what she was looking for, ''only I want it to happen again . . . now!''

She held him with both hands now, and he was hardly in a position to refuse her, even if he wanted to.

Which he most certainly didn't.

The beast watched the two humans without understanding what was going on. Their actions meant nothing at all to him. The only action that would have meant something to him was if they were to come towards him. That or daylight, whichever came first, would galvanize the great beast into action, and this was what he was waiting so patiently for.

He continued to watch, and the man lying beside him continued to snore.

Chapter Thirty-Four

"A town," Lacy said.

They were a half a day out of camp when they topped a rise and spotted it. "I didn't know there was a town here."

"Neither did I," Clint said. "It doesn't look like much of a town, though."

There were only about a half dozen ramshackle buildings, all of which looked as if they were just about ready to fall down with the first stiff wind.

"Are you sure this is the way Ol' Three-Paw came?"

"I'm sure," she said, then added, "Just as sure as I was that we were being watched last night."

"Don't remind me," Clint said.

After breaking camp Lacy had decided to ride around a bit, because she still felt sure that they were being watched all through the night. She finally found what she was looking for—bear tracks. And she also pointed something out to Clint that she had not expected to find—the tracks of a man.

"Were they both made last night?" Clint had asked.

"Hard to say for sure," she replied, "but I'd say yes."

"That grizzly's got a man traveling with him?" Clint said, incredulously. "Any sign of a horse?"

''No. If there's a man with him, he's traveling on foot.''

''Maybe this grizzly isn't as smart as we thought,'' Clint said.

''What's the difference?'' she said. ''We still don't know what that beast is going to do.''

''Maybe not,'' Clint answered, ''but if he's got a human intelligence guiding him, we've got a hell of a better chance of figuring it out.''

''And what if the human isn't guiding him?'' she asked.

''That doesn't make sense,'' Clint answered. ''Why else would a man be traveling with a grizzly?''

''I guess we'll know that when we catch up to them.''

They scattered the ashes of their campfire then, mounted up and followed the clear trail of the grizzly, until they came upon the town.

''He went around,'' she said.

''I wouldn't have expected him to go through,'' Clint said.

''No,'' she replied. ''The grizzly went around, but the man went through.''

''Then he's down there,'' Clint said. ''All we've got to do is find him. In a town that size, that shouldn't be too hard.''

''We hope,'' she said, and they started down the trail, into town.

Just before they entered they came upon a sign that told them the town was called Last Prayer, and the population figure had been crossed out and changed many times until it was down to twelve.

They sat there staring at the sign until Lacy said, ''Last Prayer. Jesus!''

"Let's hope it's not," Clint said, and they rode in.

With hills on all sides, the town of Last Prayer looked as if it had been built in a hole or at the bottom of a bowl.

"I hope they've got a saloon," Lacy said, as they rode down the main—and only—street.

"I don't think we've got to worry about that," he said. "If a town had only one building, it's a safe bet that it would be a saloon."

As they reached the center of the little town, Clint's words were proven right. Not only did the town have a saloon, but it was situated in the sturdiest looking building of the lot. As they dismounted Lacy secured Clicker's reins to a hitching post, while Clint simply dropped Duke's reins to the ground.

"Aren't you going to tie him?" she questioned.

"He's not going anywhere without me," Clint assured her. Lacy shrugged and followed Clint to the batwing doors of the saloon.

The saloon was small and empty. Against the back wall a long board sitting on two barrels acted as a bar, and behind it were two shelves with a few dusty bottles sitting on it. Also behind it was a sleepy looking man who brightened a bit when they walked in.

"Come in, come in, friends," he said cheerfully. "Welcome to Last Prayer, Wyoming. What can I get you?"

They approached the bar and Clint asked, "What's in those bottles?"

"Finest sippin' whiskey in the county, my friend," the man replied.

"Do you have any beer?" Lacy asked.

"Now, what kind of a saloon would I be running if I didn't have any beer, little lady?" the man asked.

"Is that a yes or a no?" Clint asked.

"That's a yes, friend," the man said. "Can I get you some?"

"Bring us two," Clint answered, "and I hope they're cold."

"They're as cold as I can get them."

Which turned out to be lukewarm but at least it was wet.

"Staying in town long?" the man asked. "We got us a fine little hotel."

"Do tell," Lacy said, dubiously.

"Yes, ma'am," he went on. "Fine accommodations."

"We're just passing through," Clint said, "looking for someone."

"And who might that be?"

"We don't know yet," Lacy replied. "Have you seen any strangers in town today?"

"Nobody's come into town in weeks but you two," the man said. " 'Cept maybe him," he added, pointing past them.

Both of them turned around to see who the bartender was pointing to, because they both had thought the saloon was empty. They were surprised to find that there was a man seated at a corner table with a bottle of whiskey, whom neither of them had noticed.

"I thought you said no strangers had come into town but us," Lacy asked.

"That's right, I did," he answered, "but that ain't no stranger, that's just ol' Dusty."

Clint and Lacy looked at each other, and then Clint said, "His name is Dusty?"

"Dusty," the bartender said. "Joe Dusty, Dusty Joe, but most of the time he just answers to Dusty."

Chapter Thirty-Five

Clint and Lacy took their beers and walked over to the corner table where Dusty was sitting.

The man had long black hair streaked with gray—or dust, they couldn't be sure which—and it hung loose on his shoulders. On the table was a black hat with a feather in the band. His face was weather-beaten, which made it hard to guess his age, which could have been anywhere between thirty and sixty. He was a slight man with narrow, bony shoulders; he couldn't have been more than five and a half feet tall.

"Dusty?" Lacy said, but the man showed no sign of having heard her. He was sitting with the half-filled bottle in one hand, and a glass in the other.

"Are you Dusty?" Clint said, touching one of the man's shoulders.

Slowly the man raised his eyes until he was looking at both of them. His eyes were the clearest blue either Clint or Lacy had ever seen. They were grossly out of place on the man's face.

"My name is Dusty," he said in a soft voice.

"We've been looking for you, Dusty," Clint said. "Do you mind if we sit with you?"

"Sit," the half-breed said.

They each pulled out a chair and sat with the man between them.

"Why do you seek Dusty?"

"We need your help," Clint said.

"My help?" the man asked. "Why do you need my help? What can I do for you?"

"You can help us find Ol' Three-Paw," Lacy said.

"Ah," Dusty said, nodding his head. "You seek the great grizzly bear."

"Yes," Clint said.

"For what purpose?"

"To kill him," Lacy said.

"Why?"

"For money," Lacy answered, without hesitation.

"And you?" Dusty said, turning his gaze on the Gunsmith. "Do you also seek to kill the great grizzly for money?"

"I have other reasons," Clint said.

"Ah," the half-breed said again. He turned his attention to the whiskey in his glass, which he drank, and then refilled it from the bottle.

"What would you have me do?" he asked then.

"Lead us to him," Clint said.

"I do not know where he is."

"But you could find him," Clint said. "You could track him for us."

"Yes," Dusty said. "I could, but why should I?"

"For money," Lacy said.

"Ah, the reward," Dusty said.

"We would collect the reward," Lacy hastened to explain, "but we would pay you well out of it."

"How will you kill him?"

"With this gun," Lacy said, indicating the Parker-Hale in Clint's hand. When Clint didn't raise it, Dusty leaned over so that he could examine it.

"I have never seen such a gun," Dusty said. "Ol'

Three-Paw is very large. Will this gun kill him?''

"As long as I can get close enough to make a killing shot," Clint replied.

"We must get close enough to kill him before he can kill us, right?" Dusty asked.

"Right."

Dusty nodded, drank his whiskey and refilled the glass. Clint assumed that the half-breed had started with a full bottle, and now it was three-quarters gone, but the man was showing no ill effects. That was not what he had been given to understand. Perhaps the whiskey was so liberally watered here that it would take much more than one bottle to make a man drunk.

"What do you say, Dusty?" Lacy asked. She no longer took the idea as an insult to her own trackng abilities. If the half-breed could help them get the job over and done with faster, then she was all for it.

Dusty turned his clear blue eyes on each of them in turn, as if he were looking not only at them, but deep inside of them.

"I will go with you," he said.

"Good—" Lacy began.

"After I finish my whiskey," he added, and up-ended the bottle to pour himself another drink.

Chapter Thirty-Six

Deciding not to push him, they waited patiently while Dusty finished the last of the whiskey. The final drink was in the glass when the batwing doors opened and four men stepped through, to the delight of the bartender.

Clint, however, was not so delighted.

"What's wrong?" Lacy asked.

"I don't know," he replied.

She turned her head to look in the direction of the four men, then asked, "Do you know them?"

"No," he said. "They just don't feel right. The sooner we get out of here, the better."

The men advanced on the bar while the bartender greeted them in the same cheerful matter he had greeted Clint and Lacy.

"What'll it be, friends?"

"Whiskey," one of them said.

All four were dressed in worn trail clothes, and they all wore their handguns low. When they were served one of them tasted the whiskey and then spit it out.

"This stuff tastes like buffalo piss," he complained.

One of his friends laughed and said, "When was the last time you tasted buffalo piss, Harley?"

The other man's laughter was cut short by the back

of Harley's hand, which nearly took his head off and knocked him off his feet.

"I didn't mean nothing, Harley," the fallen man mumbled, wiping blood from his face with the back of his own hand.

"You never do, Mace," Harley said.

As Harley started to turn back to the bar his eyes fell on Lacy Blake's red hair and the impressive swell of her breasts, and he stopped short.

"Whoeee!" he exclaimed loudly, and his friends turned to look also—even Mace, who was still on the floor.

"Trouble," Clint said softly. Lacy heard him, but Dusty seemed intent on his last glass of whiskey.

"If that there is your saloon girl, bartender, it just might make up for your lousy whiskey," Harley said.

"Uh, sir—" the bartender started.

"I just may let you keep your teeth, friend," Harley added, and the bartender shut his mouth and made himself as small as possible.

Harley walked over to the table where Lacy sat with Clint and Dusty and said, "Hello, pretty lady."

Lacy looked up at Harley, and the big man thought that she was even prettier than he had hoped.

"How about joining me for a drink?" he invited.

"I'm sorry," Lacy said, "but I was just getting ready to leave."

"Aw, now that ain't very friendly," Harley said. "One little drink ain't gonna hurt you—and maybe one little snuggle, huh?"

"Sorry."

"No, no," Harley said with exaggerated patience, "you don't understand. That bartender loses all of his teeth if you don't come with me."

The bartender gave a frightened squeak, but Lacy simply said, "That's his problem for letting you in here in the first place."

"You've got spirit," Harley said. "I like that. You've got big tits too," he added, "and I like that too."

He went to put one big hand on her left breast, but Lacy shifted and drove her elbow into the man's exposed stomach. He grunted, and took a few steps backward, but didn't seem any the worse for wear for the blow.

"Spirit," he said, rubbing his stomach. "Come on, Red, I'll put the boots to you like you've never had it before."

"With what?" she asked, sneering at him.

"Bitch," he said, standing straight. "You're asking for it."

"Look, friend," Lacy said, "all I'm asking is to be left alone with my friends."

"Your friends?" the man said. "A half-breed and a saddle tramp? Come on, baby, you can do better than that with me and my friends."

"I could do better than *that*," she said, "with a pack of coyotes."

"Now, look—" Harley said, but he took just one step forward when the Gunsmith spoke up.

"Drop it, friend," Clint said. "Just forget it. The lady isn't interested."

"I didn't ask you, friend," Harley said.

"But I'm telling you," Clint said. "Drink your drink and walk out. That's a friendly warning."

Harley stared at Clint for a few moments, gave Lacy a hungry look, then retreated to the bar where he and his friends had a heated discussion.

"Let's get out of here," Clint said, touching Dusty's elbow.

The three of them started to rise when Harley called out, "I don't think you'll be leaving just yet, friend."

Clint straightened up and looked towards the bar, where Harley and his three friends had spread out within arm's length of each other. The bartender was nowhere to be seen, so Clint assumed he had ducked down behind the bar.

"We're going to walk out of here," Clint told Harley, "and I wouldn't advise you to try and stop us."

"I'm gonna stop the lady," Harley said, "but I'm gonna kill you and the breed."

"Then do it," Clint said.

The other three men were keying on Harley, and when he went for his gun, they went for theirs a split second later. That split second gave Clint all the time he needed.

He drew his gun and shot Harley in the stomach, right where Lacy had planted her elbow. As the big man folded with a shocked look on his face, Clint swiveled and shot the two men standing on Harley's right. As he turned to the man's left he saw that the fourth man was already falling to the floor with a bullet from Lacy's gun in his chest.

Clint holstered his gun as the bartender stuck his head up over the bar.

"Is it over?"

"It's over," Clint said. "And not one broken glass."

Chapter Thirty-Seven

They left the town of Last Prayer with the half-breed, Dusty, on foot. They offered to buy him a horse, but he insisted that he didn't need one.

Just outside of town Ol' Three-Paw's tracks were so clear that even Clint was able to pick them up. They followed them until it was nearly dark, and then camped. Dusty sat far from Clint and Lacy, in the dark, and declined to share their food.

"He's a strange one, all right," Clint said.

"Yes," Lacy said, staring into the fire.

"More coffee?" Clint asked.

"Thanks."

He handed her the coffee, and she held it in both hands, still staring into the fire.

"What is it?" he asked.

"Huh?"

"Are you upset over last night?"

"Oh, no," she said, "never about that."

"Then what?" he asked. "You've been quiet ever since we left Last Prayer. Do you get like this every time you kill a man?"

"No," she said. "Especially not men like that."

"Then what's bothering you?"

"It's silly."

"Tell me."

"Well," she said, staring into her coffee now, "what happened back there—" She broke off and looked directly at him. "I've never seen anyone move so fast, Clint. I barely had time to draw my gun and kill the fourth man. If I hadn't, I think you would have killed him too. Four men, and you outdrew them all!"

"And that bothers you?"

"It doesn't bother me," she said. "Not really. It's just . . . it's like I've only now realized who you are."

"I'm Clint Adams."

"You're the Gunsmith," she said. "A legend, like Wild Bill Hickok."

"I'm no legend."

"You are."

"I'm not," he insisted. "The Gunsmith, *he's* a legend, but I'm not."

"But you *are* the Gunsmith."

"Not the one you've read about, or heard about," he argued. "That man doesn't exist." She stared at him for a few moments, and he said, "You don't understand, do you?"

"Yes, I think I do understand," she said. "Jake has a rep that he says is only half deserved."

"A reputation is just a lie that everyone believes," Clint said. "It does all harm, and no good."

"You would know better than I would," she conceded.

"I suppose."

"Still," she went on, "I've heard how fast you were, but I never dreamed anyone could be that fast."

"Fear does that to you," he said.

"You don't expect me to believe that," she said. "I believe you when you say you're afraid of Ol' Three-Paw but not of another man with a gun."

"Why not?" he asked. "One could kill me just as easily as the other."

She stared at him, wondering if he really meant it. She had seen no sign of fear in him while he was facing the four men in the saloon, but did that mean that it wasn't there?

Clint looked over at Dusty, who was sitting silently with his legs crossed, and Lacy asked, "What are you thinking?"

"Remember how I had the feeling those men in the saloon were trouble, before any of them even spoke?"

"Yes."

"Well, I may be wrong," he said, staring at Dusty, "but I'm starting to get the same feeling about him."

Chapter Thirty-Eight

"You didn't talk about your feelings about Dusty very much last night," Lacy said to Clint the next morning. The half-breed had gotten up earlier than they did, and was apparently out scouting for tracks.

Either that, or he'd taken off on them.

"I can't explain it, Lacy," Clint said, "but I've had an itch in the back of my neck since we picked him up yesterday."

"It was your idea," she reminded him.

"I know, I'm not arguing that," he said. "But I hadn't met him yet. He's too quiet, even for an Indian. Have you seen his eyes?"

She shrugged and said, "They're blue."

"He looks like he's in another world," Clint said.

"Too much whiskey," she suggested.

"That's another thing," he said. "The bartender back in Bear Pass told me that Dusty gets mean when he's liquored up. Did he look mean to you, yesterday?"

"No," she said. "He didn't even flinch during the gunfight. Maybe it takes more than one bottle to make him mean."

"Something's wrong," Clint insisted. "He almost

looks like he's having a religious experience all the time.''

''You can't fault a man for his reli—''

''Shh, here he comes.''

Dusty came walking back into camp and saw Clint pouring a cup of coffee for Lacy. They were both too quiet, though, and the breed surmised that they had been talking about him. No matter, he thought, they could talk all they wanted. It would not save them from the Great One.

''Good morning, Dusty,'' Lacy greeted him. ''Would you like a cup of coffee?''

''Don't drink coffee,'' the half-breed mumbled.

''What did you find this morning?'' Clint asked, settling back on his haunches with his cup of coffee.

''Tracks,'' Dusty answered, ''still going north.''

''How far ahead of us is he?''

''Hard to say,'' Dusty said, crouching down by the fire.

Lacy took the opportunity to study the man's eyes and saw what Clint had meant. There was a faraway look there, as if Dusty were seeing something other than what was right in front of him.

Suddenly, though, those eyes focused and looked directly at her and she hurriedly looked away, into the fire, feeling her face flush at the same time.

''Do I interest you?'' she heard Dusty ask.

''I didn't mean to stare,'' she said, covering up as best she could, ''but you have very . . . unusual eyes.''

''The eyes mirror the soul,'' Dusty said, and looked away from her.

Lacy looked at Clint across the fire and gave a little involuntary shiver.

"We should move before he gets too far ahead," Dusty told Clint.

"You're right," Clint said. He took one last sip of his coffee and dumped the rest of it into the fire. Lacy followed his example, and Dusty stood up and kicked sand on the fire, to finally douse it.

"Let's go," Clint said.

Lacy took the utensils and stowed them in her saddlebag, and they mounted up as Dusty started off on foot.

"The man doesn't get tired," Lacy said as she and Clint started after him.

"Yeah," Clint said, "that's another thing."

Dusty was running steadily ahead of the two massive horses, breathing easily with no feeling of fatigue at all. Even when they had stopped to camp, he had felt no fatigue. He was in the service of the Great One, who would not allow him to feel fatigue.

It would have been so easy for him to have killed the two people while they slept, slitting their throats from ear to ear with his knife and then waiting for the Great One to come down and sate himself on their flesh and blood, but that was not the way the Great One wanted it. Dusty Joe was the great grizzly's servant, and he would continue to do things just the way the Great One wanted him to.

Yes, he answered as the call came to him, *I'm coming, Great One, and I am bringing them to you.*

Chapter Thirty-Nine

By the end of the day, Clint was convinced that something was going on with Dusty Joe. As they camped, he sent the half-breed for water at the nearby stream so that he could talk to Lacy alone.

"Have you noticed something?" Clint asked.

"Like what?"

"You're a tracker, Lacy," Clint said. "You must have noticed something wrong with the way Dusty is tracking Ol' Three-Paw."

"He's doing it a lot faster that I could have," she admitted, "though it pains me to admit it."

"Too fast, Lacy," Clint insisted. He kept an eye out for Dusty and decided to give it to her straight. "Lacy, he knows where he's going."

"What?"

"If he's following a trail, it has to be about five and a half feet off the ground," Clint said.

"Are you sure?"

"I've been watching him," Clint said. "The only time he looks down is to make sure he doesn't spit on his feet. I understand in some circles it's considered bad luck."

"But where is he taking us?" she asked.

"That's a good question," he answered. "And one almost as good is, why?"

"A trap," Lacy said.

"Again, why?" Clint asked. "What have either one of us done to him?"

Lacy cocked an eyebrow at Clint and said, "Between us we've killed a lot of people, Clint. Who's to say that Dusty's not related to one of them?"

"If his aim is to kill us, he could have done it at night, during his watch," Clint said.

"No, he couldn't have," Lacy answered. "To tell you the truth, I didn't sleep too well last night—at least, not while he was on watch."

"I didn't, either," Clint also admitted.

"But he just sat there," she said. "He never looked over at either one of us."

"I can't figure it—" Clint began to say, but the appearance of Dusty Joe cut him short.

"How's the stream?" Clint asked.

"Fine."

"Is it deep enough to take a bath?" Lacy asked.

The half-breed looked at her for a few seconds, and then said, "It is deep enough."

She looked at Clint, who nodded and said, "Sure, go ahead."

She gave him a long glance, which he took to mean that she wished he could go with her, and he gave her a small smile, which meant that he wished he could too.

"I won't be long," she promised.

"Take your time," he said. "Just get back before it gets dark. I'll have the coffee ready."

She smiled and started toward the stream.

Lacy left her clothes on a large, flat rock and waded into the stream naked. The water was cool, refreshing, and it came to her waist.

She caught the water in her cupped hands and let it pour down over her breasts. The coolness of it hardened her nipples, and thinking of Clint Adams she rubbed her palms over her nipples in circular motions, stimulating them further.

Her thoughts were all of Clint Adams now. It was the first time she had ever had sex with someone she rode with. She had been riding with Jake Benteen for three years, and they had never even come close to being in the same bed together. Why had she broken her rule with this man? Was it only because of the fear she had felt, or was it something else? Why did she feel so different when she was with him?

She ran her hands over her breasts, down across her stomach, and then into the water, between her legs. Her eyes were closed and her head was thrown back and as she rubbed herself she fervently wished that Clint were there with her.

She started to shiver then, either from the water or from her need, and she opened her eyes to leave the stream. As she did and lowered her head, she saw him, standing up on his hind legs, incredibly large and powerful, watching her. As he placed one paw into the water, she opened her mouth to scream. . . .

Clint placed the coffeepot over the flame and looked at Dusty Joe.

"Who are you, Joe?" he asked, on impulse. "Or better yet, *what* are you? Why did you come along with us?"

"Three questions," Dusty said. "Which would you like me to answer first?"

Clint grinned and said, "All three, but in any order you like."

"I am who I am," the half-breed said. "A half-breed called Dusty Joe. My mother was a white woman, my father was a Comanche medicine man, a shaman. I am . . . a half-breed," he said, answering the second question with a fatalistic shrug. "That is all anyone will let me be."

"All right," Clint said. "How about the last question?"

"Why I came along?" Dusty said. "Miss Lacy could answer that for you."

"She'd say the money."

"And what would you say?"

"I don't know, exactly," Clint said. "But I'd say something else, not the money."

"Maybe I just didn't have anything better to do," Dusty Joe suggested. "Would you accept that?"

The Gunsmith didn't have a chance to say whether he would or wouldn't, because at that moment, Lacy Blake screamed.

Clint grabbed up the Parker-Hale and didn't stop to see if Dusty Joe would follow him. He ran through the brush, dreading what he might find when he reached the stream.

The first thing he saw when he approached the stream was Lacy's clothes, laid out on the flat rock. He felt a moment of panic, and then saw her, staggering from the stream, rivulets of water running down her naked skin.

"Lacy!"

"Clint," she shouted, running to him. She ran into his arms and he didn't even notice that she was soaking his clothes as he put his arms around her.

"What happened?"

"He was there, Clint," she said. "Ol' Three-Paw was there."

"Where, honey? Where?"

"There," she answered, pointing to the opposite bank of the stream. "He was watching me bathe, and then he started into the water, and I screamed."

Clint barely heard a sound behind him, and then Dusty Joe was standing next to them. The half-breed seemed totally oblivious of Lacy's nakedness, which was just one more strange thing about the man to add to the list.

"Get your clothes on," Clint told Lacy. To Dusty Joe he said, "Stay with her."

"Where are you going?" she asked, clutching his shirt.

"I'm going to see if I can catch up to him."

"That is foolish," the half-breed said.

"Why?" Clint asked.

"A grizzly bear moves faster than most men think," Dusty Joe answered, "especially one that size."

"He's missing a paw," Clint reminded him.

"He can still run faster than you can," Dusty Joe insisted. "Especially by the time you wade across that stream."

"What do you suggest, then?"

"It is getting dark," Joe said. "You would be helpless stumbling around in the dark. I suggest we go back to camp, and in the morning we will pick up his trail. We are very close now, and with your horses you may be able to close the gap."

"What about you?" Clint asked, as Lacy moved to the flat rock and started getting dressed. "You don't have a horse. How will you keep up?"

"I am half Comanche," he said, proudly, as if that answered the question sufficiently.

"He's right, Clint," Lacy said, strapping on her gun. "You wouldn't have a chance in the dark."

"Yeah," Clint said, hefting the Parker-Hale. "I know."

"Let us go back to camp," Dusty Joe said. "The coffee will be very strong."

Both Clint and Lacy looked at the little half-breed, as if unsure that they had heard him right.

"I think that two of us should stay awake tonight," Dusty Joe said, by way of explanation. "Isn't that one of the functions of coffee?"

Lacy looked at Clint, who shrugged and said, "Let's go back to camp and find out."

Chapter Forty

Dusty Joe refused to sleep that night, so that either Clint or Lacy would always be asleep, while the other sat up with the half-breed. At one point, Clint decided that he would have preferred sitting up with Lacy while Dusty slept. It was unnerving to sit there with the half-breed simply staring out into the darkness as if he were in some sort of trance.

As they started out the next morning, Dusty went on ahead of them to scout, while Clint and Lacy walked their horses, taking advantage of the opportunity to talk without Dusty around.

"I've never seen anything like it," Lacy said, when Clint asked her to describe the bear she saw. "He was beautiful and grotesque at the same time."

"Are you sure it was Ol' Three-Paw?"

"That's what was grotesque," she said. "The stump of that fourth paw."

"What about the gray streak?" he asked.

"What?"

"Did the bear you saw have a streak of gray hair on his right shoulder?"

"I—I didn't notice that," she said. "I'm sorry, Clint."

"That's all right."

"That's the second time you've asked me that," she said. "Why is it important?"

"It's not," he assured her. "It's just something somebody told me."

Looking ahead of them for Dusty Joe, Lacy said, "I wonder where he went now."

"Scouting for tracks, he says," Clint replied, "but I'm not all that sure he needs to."

"What do you mean?" she asked, looking puzzled. "Doesn't the fact that Ol' Three-Paw is so close shoot down your theory that Dusty isn't leading us somewhere else?"

"Not necessarily," Clint said. "Maybe Dusty Joe is leading us right to Ol' Three-Paw."

"Isn't that what we want?"

"That may be what we think we want," he answered.

"I'm not following you."

"Have you looked at Dusty Joe's tracks?"

"*His* tracks?"

"Pull up for a moment."

"We'll lose Dusty."

"Don't worry," Clint said. "I have a feeling he'll make sure he doesn't lose us. Pull up."

They both reined in and Clint got down. Lacy followed his example and stared at him, feeling more and more puzzled.

"Look at Dusty's tracks," he instructed her.

She stared at him a moment longer, to be sure she heard him right, then looked down and found some of the half-breed's tracks in the loose dirt.

"So?"

"Have you seen tracks like those before?"

"He's wearing moccasins," she said. "I've been

through Indian country once or twice, Clint.''

"I mean recently," he said. "Like on a rise that overlooked one of our campsites a few nights ago."

She looked at him for a few moments, still not understanding, and then suddenly her face changed as it dawned on her.

"You mean that morning we found Ol' Three-Paw's tracks, and the tracks of a man?" she asked.

"Right."

"You think Dusty Joe has been traveling with that big grizzly?" she asked.

"It's possible," he said.

"Then you think he and the bear are leading us on, until—"

"Until we reach a certain spot where Ol' Three-Paw will turn and face us."

"But why?" she asked. "Why would he travel with a bear? Why would he risk being killed—hell, why hasn't the bear killed him?"

"All good questions," Clint said. "We have two choices, Lacy. We can go that way," he said, pointing, "and find out the answers, or we can go that way"— he pointed behind them— "and forget the whole thing."

Lacy actually looked in each direction, as if she were considering the options, and then said, "That way means money to me," she said, "and going back means nothing. I'm not going back with nothing, Clint. I'm going back with that grizzly's ears."

She pulled Clicker around and mounted up.

"You can go back if you want to, but I'm going on."

Clint climbed up onto Duke's back and said, "Lacy, I'd never forgive myself if I did."

● ● ●

Dusty Joe ran on, knowing full well that Clint Adams and Lacy Blake would follow. His mind was on the one the whites called Ol' Three-Paw. The Great One had allowed himself to be seen by the woman. This was the sign that Dusty Joe needed to tell him that it was time.

The Great One would have his nourishment—today!

It was past midday and they still had not seen any sign of Dusty Joe returning. They stopped only once to rest the horses, because the heat of the day was oppressive, and they had decided that resting the animals was more important than arguing over which needed it more than the other.

"We could be in Montana in a few hours," Lacy said during the rest stop.

"That will bring us right back to where it all started," Clint said, thinking of Dorian Ward.

"What do you mean?"

"Just something somebody told me," he said again, and Lacy, although she was curious, respected his right to explain or not.

Later she said, "You know, if he doesn't come back at all, it shoots another theory all to hell."

"You mean about him leading us to where Ol' Three-Paw wants us?"

"Right."

"No, it doesn't."

"How do you figure?"

"If he doesn't come back," Clint said, "it means we're already here."

Dusty Joe stopped running when he saw the Great One up ahead, standing straight up, waiting. The grizzly was at the base of a cliff, and just behind him

Dusty could see the mouth of a cave.

"I understand, Great One," he said aloud. The grizzly seemed to paw at the air with the stump of his missing paw, and Dusty said again, "I understand."

This was where the Great One wanted the two whites, this was where he would take their blood and their hearts.

"Yes, my Father," Dusty Joe said, "I understand."

When they finally spotted Dusty Joe coming towards them, it was an hour before dark. They reined their horses in and waited for him to come to them.

"Where the hell have you been all day?" Clint demanded.

"You wanted me to find . . . Ol' Three-Paw," Dusty said, pausing just before he named the grizzly.

"So?"

"I have found him."

"You found him?" Lacy said.

"Yes."

"Take us to him," Clint said, giving Lacy a sidelong glance that she returned. "Take us to him, Dusty."

"That is what I intend to do," Dusty Joe assured them.

So they both followed Dusty Joe, knowing full well that he may have been—and probably was—leading them into some sort of trap.

Lacy Blake had her reasons, and in the beginning they were all green—money! Clint Adams was a large part of her reason, now. They had come this far together, and she wanted to finish it the same way.

The Gunsmith had reasons other than money all

along—Dorian Ward, and then Hank Pride, and yes, to a lesser degree, money—but now he had an entirely different reason: Lacy Blake. Clint knew that if he turned back now, Lacy would insist on going on alone. Without his Parker-Hale, she wouldn't have a chance against that monster, and he couldn't very well leave her the gun, could he? Who knew if he'd ever get it back again?

So the Gunsmith reasoned that he was following Dusty Joe and Lacy Blake because she needed the Parker-Hale to have any hope of downing Ol' Three-Paw, and just as soon as that was done, they would go their separate ways.

If they were still alive.

Chapter Forty-One

It was nearly dark when they reached the mouth of the cave at the base of the cliff.

"I don't like this," Clint said to Lacy in low tones.

"Neither do I," she said. "You don't suppose he's going to tell us that Ol' Three-Paw is in there?"

"The entrance is certainly big enough," Clint said, "but I don't know—"

Dusty came walking up to them and cut short whatever Clint was going to say.

"You can see the tracks for yourself," Dusty said, pointing to the ground in front of the mouth of the cave. "It is covered with tracks."

"How can you be sure they belong to Ol' Three-Paw?" Lacy asked.

He looked up at Lacy with those flat, expressionless eyes, and said, "There is no other grizzly that big."

Clint dismounted and grabbed the Parker-Hale. The feel of its weight should have been something of a comfort, but it wasn't.

"What do you suggest, Dusty?" Clint asked.

"I have been inside."

"You went in there alone?" Lacy asked.

"You wish me to earn my money, right?" he asked. "I went in and there are many caverns. You would get lost," he said, speaking to both of them.

"Then what's your suggestion?"

"I will go in, find him, and drive him out to you," Dusty said.

Clint and Lacy exchanged disbelieving glances. That a man—any man, let alone someone Dusty's size—could drive a ten to twelve foot grizzly out of its lair was hard to swallow.

"How do you plan to do that?"

"With fire," Dusty said. "I will make a torch, which will serve two purposes. It will light my way, and it will drive the grizzly out of its lair. An animal, no matter what size it is, fears fire."

He looked at both of them, waiting for their answer.

"I can't come up with anything better," Clint said, "and he's got a point about the fire."

"So then we'll wait," Lacy said, shrugging her shoulders.

"We've tracked the beast to its lair," Dusty said. "Now all that need be done is drive him out, and he's yours."

"I hope so," Lacy said.

Clint fingered the Parker-Hale and said, "I guess we'd better find a torch."

"I have one," Dusty said. He went to the mouth of the cave and picked something up from behind a bunch of rocks. For some kind of spur of the moment, makeshift torch, it looked pretty damned efficient.

"I made it earlier," Dusty explained. "Do you have something to light it with?"

Clint produced a lucifer and flicked it to life with his thumbnail. He touched the flame to the torch, and it burst to life.

Dusty looked up and said, "Darkness is not far away. If the grizzly does not come out, and I do not come out by then, one of you will have to follow, while the other waits. If the second one does not return, it is up to the survivor what he or she will do next.''

''We understand,'' Clint said.

Dusty nodded and turned to the mouth of the cave.

''Good luck,'' Lacy called out.

He turned and fixed his strange eyes on her, then turned back to them and entered the cave.

Darkness fell about five minutes later.

''He miscalculated,'' Lacy said, looking up.

''I wonder,'' Clint said.

''What do we do?''

''Give him some more time,'' Clint said, ''then I'll go in after him.''

''You?'' she said. ''Why you?''

He looked at her and said, ''Well, why should you go?''

''I've got just as much right to go as you have,'' she said. ''We're partners.''

''Yeah, so?'' Clint asked. ''One of us has to go, so I'll go. What's the beef?''

''What kind of a way is that for partners to decide who goes or stays?'' she demanded. ''We've got to do this so that it's fair.''

''I'll wrestle you for it,'' Clint said.

She fixed him with a hard-eyed stare and said, ''Don't be so sure you'd win, friend.''

''All right, all right,'' Clint said. ''What do you suggest?''

''I'll go in and you stay.''

''How's that fair?''

She gave him a wan smile and said, ''Ladies first.''

Chapter Forty-Two

Ladies first did not quite decide it.

Clint finally had to give in because Lacy Blake put on her bounty hunter face, and he had to remind himself that a man like Jake Benteen trusted this woman enough to make her his partner three years ago.

They drew straws, and when Lacy won she gave him a satisfied smirk.

"I don't know how Jake Benteen put up with you for three years," he said in disgust.

"Don't get sore," she said, looking around for something to make a torch out of. She finally settled for a large tree limb, wrapped with brush and her bandana. Clint produced a leather thong to tie it all off with, and then supplied another lucifer.

"That thing is not going to last long, Lacy," he warned. "If you don't find that grizzly in a few minutes, come on back out. We'll think of something else."

"I'll drive him right into your lap, Clint," she assured him. "You just keep that big rifle of yours handy."

He was going to offer the Parker-Hale to her, but she was right about one thing. When and if that grizzly came charging out, it would be into his lap, and his modified .45 just wouldn't do it.

"Honey," he told her seriously, "be careful. Don't get cute and don't try anything. Just send him out to me."

"Don't worry," she said, drawing her gun. "I'll put a couple in his ass on his way out."

She kissed him quickly on the mouth, and then hurried to the mouth of the cave before she changed her mind.

After she had gone ten feet Lacy saw what Dusty Joe had meant when he said they could get lost. From where she stood she could see that the cave branched off in three different directions. Picking one would have been a monumental decision if it had not been for the fact that Dusty Joe had left a trail for them to follow.

The half-breed appeared to have dragged his torch along the floor of the cave, leaving a scorch line to mark his progress. Holding her torch up in front of her, she set off after Dusty Joe. He hadn't returned, so he must have gone the right way, and gotten killed.

Unless Clint's theory was right. What if Dusty Joe was working with the grizzly? But how could that be? Why would a wild beast ally itself with a man?

Or vice versa?

Holding the torch firmly in her left hand, and her .45 in her right, she pressed on, trying not to think of what was ahead, ready to accept and deal with whatever came.

Outside the Gunsmith spared a few moments to fashion a makeshift torch of his own, then positioned himself so that he could not miss the grizzly charging out of the cave even if he wanted to. He cocked both hammers on the Parker-Hale, and waited.

He did not fashion or light a second torch, for fear that the grizzly would see it; and who was to say that there was only one grizzly? If this was Ol' Three-Paw's lair, who was to say that he didn't have a family inside—a Mrs. Three-Paw and little Three-Paw kiddies?

The two-shot Parker-Hale suddenly seemed a less formidable weapon. From his pocket he took extra rounds, and laid them on the ground in front of him. He gathered his legs underneath him in a crouch and held the big weapon in both hands, pointing at the mouth of the cave. He didn't even want to give the grizzly a chance to step out. The light of the nearly full moon was all he'd need to spot the giant grizzly, and put two quick shots into him, then reload before assessing the damage.

Clint allowed a certain amount of time to go by, and then decided that he had let too much time go by. He had waited too long. He pocketed the extra rounds for the Parker-Hale, picked up his torch, and stood up, stretching his cramped knees. He produced a third lucifer, lit his torch, hefted the Parker-Hale, and prepared to go inside, where Dusty Joe and Lacy Blake had gone before him, and from where neither had returned.

Chapter Forty-Three

Clint stuck the torch in ahead of him, looked over the cavern and then stepped in. As large and heavy as the big game gun was in his hand, he had the feeling that he would have felt more secure with his modified Colt .45 in hand. That gun had saved his life countless times. He could not quite accept the idea that it would not do the job this time.

Turning those thoughts aside, he held the Parker-Hale tight and started walking. He had gone ten feet when he came to that three-way fork. Like Lacy before him, he spotted the scorch line on the floor. They both went that way, he thought, and didn't come out. Were they dead?

Was Lacy dead?

If she was, it was because she went that way.

Clint examined the other two tunnels, only one of which—the one on the far right—was large enough to allow Ol' Three-Paw to enter. The middle one had only a small crack as an entrance, large enough for a man, but not for a grizzly.

He went that way.

He had to turn sideways, put the torch ahead of him and the Parker-Hale behind him, but once he was inside the cavern widened, and he was able to walk.

From what he had seen of the first tunnel, he guessed

that this one would run parallel with it, maybe for a while, but maybe all the way. Ol' Three-Paw wouldn't use it because the entrance was too small, and maybe this already put him one up on the big grizzly.

He walked on, listening intently for the slightest sound ahead of him, or behind him. Dusty Joe could fit through that crack, and if he was alive and working with the grizzly—for God only knew what reason— he'd have to be careful the half-breed didn't injun up behind him.

Suddenly, his torch flared, and then died, and at the same moment he felt a breeze and heard voices. The breeze was strong enough to have blown out his torch, but it was also strong enough to carry the voices with it.

He continued on in the dark, following the sound of the voices, holding the Parker-Hale tightly in both hands.

Finally, he saw some light ahead, streaming through a small crack, just like the entrance crack he had come through. He hurried to it and looked through.

Dusty Joe was standing in the center of what appeared to be an altar, but he was no longer Dusty Joe the half-breed. Wearing only a loincloth, the breed now looked full-blooded Indian, with some sort of design painted on his chest. On his head he wore a large set of buffalo horns, the kind you might expect a medicine man to wear. Clint remembered Dusty telling him that his father had been a medicine man.

Behind Dusty stood Lacy Blake, totally, breathtakingly naked; she was tied to the altar and her body had been smeared with oils, making it gleam in the light of the large, twin torches on either side of the altar. Clint was about to step through into the cavern when Lacy spoke.

"Why are you doing this?" she asked Dusty, and from the tone of her voice, Clint could tell it was not the first time she had asked. He stood still, wanting to hear the answer.

"I will tell you," Dusty said after a moment, turning to face her. As had been the case by the stream, he did not seem the least bit aroused by her nakedness.

Clint could not say the same for himself, despite the circumstances.

"The Great One commands it."

"What great one?" Lacy asked. "That grizzly? What is he to you, some kind of God? Dusty, you're crazy—"

"He is my God," Dusty shouted, "and he carries the soul of my father within him. I must do as he commands, always."

"Dusty," Lacy said, her tone softer now, "when did this start?"

"The Great One came to Wyoming from Montana, and sought me out," Dusty said. "I was the first one to see him, and welcome him, but others did not welcome him. They tried to kill him, and we brought them here."

He turned his head, and both Clint and Lacy followed with their eyes. They saw a pile of bones and skulls in one corner.

"They were brave, as were you and your companion," Dusty went on. "He fed on their flesh, their blood, and their hearts, as he will feed on yours, and on Clint Adams's."

"Clint is gone, Dusty," Lacy said. "He must have left when we didn't return."

"He will come," Dusty said confidently. "And the Great One will have his nourishment."

Clint had heard enough. He had to get Lacy out of there before the grizzly showed up—and he had no doubt that the monster would. Whatever the explanation, there seemed to be some bond between man and beast, one that could not be denied.

Clint stepped through the crack into the cavern, and Lacy was the first to see him.

Had he followed the scorched trail, he would have entered the cavern from the front, but following the other tunnel, he had now entered from the back.

"I must wait for Adams to come," Dusty said, and he started for the front tunnel, apparently to ambush Clint when he came through.

"That won't be necessary," Clint called out.

"Clint!" Lacy said, with relief. "He grabbed me from behind—"

"Silence!" Dusty shouted.

Lacy lapsed into a shocked silence, and Dusty turned his eyes towards Clint. His previously expressionless eyes now had a wild look to them. Clint had just about been right when he said that Dusty appeared to be having a religious experience.

"You have come," Dusty said. "That is good."

"I hate to disappoint you, Dusty," Clint said, "but I don't think this has gone just the way you wanted it to."

"You are here," the crazed half-breed said. "That is all that matters."

"Dusty, listen to me," Clint said. "I don't want to kill you. I don't know how you became convinced that the soul of your father exists inside Ol' Three-Paw—"

"Don't call him by that name!"

Dusty was unarmed, but showed no fear of Clint's weapons.

"Dusty—"

"Wait," the breed said, holding up one hand. Suddenly, his face lit up in a surprisingly serene smile, and he said, "He comes."

From still another cavern, Ol' Three-Paw came. Lacy's eyes widened, Dusty backed up until his back was against the wall, and Clint swung the Parker-Hale in the grizzly's direction.

The bear came into the cavern on all fours, but was massive nevertheless. He swung his giant head back and forth, and seemed to be looking at each of them in turn. His presence filled the cavern and Clint felt fear as he had never felt it before.

The grizzly limped when it put its great weight on the stump of its fourth paw. It moved farther into the cavern until it seemed dwarfed by his presence.

"Oh, shit," Clint heard Lacy say, and he couldn't have agreed more.

"They are here, O Great One," Dusty sang out, "and they are yours."

The bear looked in Dusty's direction, then directed its gaze towards Clint. The creature seemed totally relaxed, resting its weight on three paws now, with the stump of the fourth hovering in the air. Clint held the Parker-Hale, both hammers cocked, finger on the triggers.

Suddenly, the creature's muscles tensed, and it stood up. As it rose Clint watched, wondering when the great creature would reach its full height. When it did, it might have stood as much as twelve feet, but in that cavern it seemed like twenty.

Standing straight up now, the creature opened its mouth and let out a great bellow. It fixed its eyes on Clint again, and began to advance on him.

"Shoot, Clint, shoot!" Lacy screamed.

"It will do him no good," Dusty assured her.

She continued to shout at him, but Clint held back, letting the gigantic beast come closer, until he was almost overwhelmed by the stench it gave off.

The creature bellowed again and suddenly it charged, so fast that Clint almost didn't have time to fire.

He pulled the trigger, discharging one round, and watched it punch a hole in the creature's chest. The blood gushed out with such force that it washed over him, knocking him back.

Through a red haze he saw Ol' Three-Paw stagger, retain his balance, and start forward again. Desperately, Clint tried to clean the blood from his face with his sleeve, to clear his eyesight, but he gave it up as the bear kept coming closer. It was almost on top of him when he pulled the trigger on the Parker-Hale, sending the second round to plow into Ol' Three-Paw's massive bulk.

The blood gushed from the wound, which was only a hand's breadth from the first, and the great grizzly staggered back, crying out in pain and rage. Clint dragged himself to his feet, wanting to move around behind the bear and reload the Parker-Hale, but in his agony the bear lunged forward, lashing out with its good paw. He caught Clint high on the left arm and shoulder, sending the Gunsmith spinning to the cavern floor with such force that the Parker-Hale sprang loose from his grip and skittered across the floor.

"Oh, my God!" Lacy cried out. "He's not dead."

Not dead, but badly wounded, staggering about, trying to keep his balance, and at the same time trying to reach the man who had caused him all the pain he was feeling. His insides were badly torn up. One bullet had exited from the back, creating another bloody gash, and the other had imbedded itself deep inside of him, but he finally regained his balance and started towards the fallen Gunsmith.

"Run, Clint, run!" Lacy screamed.

He could have run, he realized. He probably could have made it back the way he came, where the grizzly couldn't follow him. In time the monster would have to die from those wounds, but before then would he kill Lacy? Would Dusty kill Lacy?

He couldn't run, not while Lacy was still in danger, and he couldn't reach the Parker-Hale in time, reload and fire. He was left with only one chance, and that was his .45, the gun that had pulled him out of more scrapes than he could count—but none as big as this.

As the grizzly advanced on him, Clint leaned to his left and drew his gun with his right hand. He pointed the gun at the grizzly's massive head and pulled the trigger six times. All six slugs went straight for the creature's head. Incredibly, the first slug cut a furrow over the bear's nose, between his eyes, and then glanced off its skull, but the other five found softer points of entry—one through each eye, two into the gaping, slobbering mouth, and one punched a hole in the animal's throat.

The twelve-foot monster staggered back three or four steps, and suddenly it toppled over backward, striking the floor with such force that Clint could feel the entire cavern shake.

"My God," Lacy breathed.

Clint staggered to his feet and realized that he was bleeding from the left shoulder, though not badly. He holstered the gun and clapped his hand over the claw mark.

"Clint," Lacy called.

He turned, climbed the altar and stood in front of her, struck by her incredible beauty even then.

"It's over, Lacy," he said. "Ol' Three-Paw is dead."

"Clint!" she suddenly shouted, and he turned in time to see Dusty Joe brandishing a large knife. Clint's hand streaked to his gun when he realized that it was empty. It didn't matter, though, because Dusty raised the knife, and then with a wild yell, plunged it into his own stomach.

He fell to the cavern floor, as dead as his "God."

Clint turned back to Lacy, who seemed to have had just about all she could take.

He untied her, and she slumped into his arms, breasts crushed flat against his chest, face buried in his shoulder.

"It's over," he said again, holding her. "Let's get you dressed and out of here. You've got a reward to collect."

"Clint," she said, her voice muffled against him.

"Yeah, honey?"

She raised her face so she could look at him and be heard clearly, and said, "He had a gray streak on his right shoulder."

Clint smiled wearily and said, "Thanks, honey. That's my reward."

www.ingramcontent.com/pod-product-compliance
Lightning Source LLC
Chambersburg PA
CBHW050731250626
47155CB00005B/1746